# THE GRAVITY OF LOVE

# SARA STRIDSBERG

# THE GRAVITY OF LOVE
## ODE TO MY FAMILY

*Translated from the Swedish by*
*Deborah Bragan-Turner*

MACLEHOSE PRESS
QUERCUS · LONDON

First published in the Swedish language as *Beckomberga: ode till min familj* by
Albert Bonniers förlag, Stockholm, in 2014
First published in Great Britain in 2016 by MacLehose Press
This paperback edition published in 2019 by

MacLehose Press
An imprint of Quercus Editions Limited
Carmelite House
50 Victoria Embankment
London EC4Y 0DZ

AN HACHETTE UK COMPANY

Part of the cost of this translation has been defrayed by a subsidy from the
Swedish Arts Council, gratefully acknowledged.

ISBN (MMP) 978 0 85705 478 4
ISBN (Ebook) 978 0 85705 477 7

# THE GRAVITY OF LOVE

A solitary white ocean bird glides along the corridors of the Stora Mans unit at Beckomberga Hospital. It is huge, and dazzling, and in my dream I am running in pursuit, but before I catch up, it flies out through a shattered window and disappears into the night.

# THE LAST PATIENT
## (OLOF)

The Spånga radio station mast, just outside Stockholm, late in the winter of 1995. A bleak, frozen landscape spreads out before him as he climbs up the mast in the icy wind. His body is old and frail, but inwardly he is young and brimming with strength. He keeps his eyes fixed on his hands to stop the dizziness, and all around him the night is clear: the stars, pinprick holes letting in light from another world, a powerful radiance glinting beyond the black, a promise of something else, a shimmering brightness that will sparkle and sustain him in place of the ever-seeping damp, the cold darkness of a grey sun, a gritty, grainy sunshine. On the horizon the first pale flicker of light, a thin atmospheric streak of pink and gold, and a few kilometres away, waiting for him in a dormitory at Beckomberga, his bed, empty, remade with clean sheets, alongside other beds on which the gently sleeping shapes of vulnerable bodies once lay under covers. Now, all gone.

He stands for a long time on the ledge at the very top and looks out over the darkened city and the white glimmer of occasional night-time lights. Then he takes off his coat and thick sweater, his black hospital cap and spectacles, and places everything in a neat little pile beside him. The world sprawls out beneath, a blanket of houses and streets and people breathing with one clear, firm, collective human lung; but there is no future for him in it, there never has been, he has always walked alone with the stamp of illness imprinted under his skin, visible to all apart from himself. Whenever he has approached a girl she has shied away. Every time he has offered his hand to someone it has been construed as hostile and he has been banished back to the hospital. An invisible grille has come down between him and the world; silent faces have turned away, making him wary of others, and so, gradually, he has withdrawn and kept to himself. No-one in the world will miss him and his clumsy greyness, there is nothing special connecting him to anyone in particular; he has never been naked with anyone, never touched anyone, as though he has been living under a hood of darkness, with no obligations, no human ties: only the grille, and the hidden chains holding him back and keeping him apart. When the nurse goes through the empty dormitories and turns on the lights in the last ward at Stora Mans, he throws himself out into the night with but one wish: that, even now, something will bear him aloft, a hand or a gust of wind; that something will sustain him in this world; but he is only a bundle tossed and turned in the air a couple of times before spinning over the edge of the earth, thudding into the ground, crumpling.

During the final months at Beckomberga he has been given permission to go out on his own, but he has never made use of it. Instead, he spends day after day sitting at the window look-ing at the trees; not once does he step out for a walk in the yard with the others. He stops switching on the light in the globe that has been by his bed for many years, and the day before he is due to leave the hospital, after the discharge interview with Dr Janowski, he stands outside the door to the ward sister's room, cap and coat over his pyjamas, and announces he is going off for a few hours to pick flowers. (*Pick flowers in February?*) He disappears and does not come back that evening or the next day. A few days later his body is found under the radio mast; a woman out walking her dog in the area discovers him lying on last year's yellow grass, outstretched in his striped pyjamas, his head smashed, rime frost on his clothes.

I

# THE FIRST CONVERSATION

"I saw in the paper that Edvard Winterson's dead," Jim says, as he sits in the little circle of light from my reading lamp on Jungfrugatan, fingering a newspaper clipping, a death notice. "The consultant on my ward at Beckomberga. Do you remember him, Jackie?"

As we talk the stars come out one by one in the firmament outside, a string of luminous pearls over the deep azure in the muted, muzzy light of evening, and of course I remember Edvard: standing as he did by the entrance to Stora Mans at nightfall, smoking a cigarette, a single wreath of smoke in the grey light, his wide smile when he caught sight of Jim, and how I once fell asleep on the faded cover of the back seat when he drove me home from the hospital.

In the soft lamplight Jim tells me that, during his time as a patient at Beckomberga, he would go with Edvard in his silver Mercedes to night parties in Östermalm. At sundown he would be collected from the ward and they would drive along the avenue of lime trees and on into the sleeping city that once had been his life. Edvard Winterson brought civilian clothes for him, a clean shirt, jeans and a jacket, waiting in a tidy little stack on top of the car, and by the time they swept out through the hospital gates he already had a cigarette and a drink in his hand.

"Edvard was a fantastic man," Jim says, and laughs, "and he was completely mad as well. We fell in love with the same woman. Sabina. Do you remember her? She was a wild one. And because Edvard was just a rich kid from Östermalm, he had no idea how to handle her."

⸺∞⸺

One or two straggling clouds drift over the smudged Indian ink drawing that is the sky, that first winter afternoon when Jim comes and tells me about Beckomberga. He is on one of his sporadic visits to Stockholm and in a few days he will be going back to Cariño, to his house by the Atlantic. The sun's fading red striations and the curls of smoke trailing from his mouth while he speaks make me think of the mist hanging over the district the first time Lone and I went to visit him, the wisps of snow lingering between the buildings.

Around us, as we walked along the asphalted paths trying to read the signs, everything was frozen. It looked as if someone had cut the bark off the wet tree trunks and I can still hear the magpies' shrill calls echoing between the buildings of the barrack-like yard as we hurried in the direction of Stora Mans. Lone in bright red coat and boots, leaning forward slightly, her hands holding the lapels tight, as though she were walking through a storm. Jim's pale, unsmiling face, his eyes glazed, his hands shaking so much when he tried to light a cigarette that he was forced to give up and put it aside. Lone, who had actually given up smoking, picked up the packet and lit one for him and another for herself. She took a couple of quick draws before crushing the cigarette under the heel of her boot.

*Jim: I'd tried many times before, but never very seriously. Many times, Lone came home from work to see me lying with my head in the gas oven. A bouquet of roses on the kitchen table and the gas on. Those were experiments. This time it was like being in free fall. I fell, and I carried on falling.*

Jim's friends at the hospital called him Jimmie Darling and after a while I started to call him Jimmie Darling too, when we were sitting with the other patients on the little slope surrounded by birch saplings. The smoke rising towards heaven from the cigarettes was a signal to those who were on the other side of the fence, a greeting to the world beyond. I collected the butts and gave them to Jim and Sabina and later to Paul.

"Jimmie Darling?"

"Yes."

"Will you get well again?"

"I don't know, Jackie."

"Don't you want to be well?"

"I don't know what I want anymore. I don't know what it means to be well. And I feel at home here, more at home than I've ever done anywhere else. The people here are different, they have nothing, and I've learned this: that it doesn't matter what you have or where you live – it's the same for everyone, there isn't any way to shield yourself."

"Shield yourself against what?"

"I don't know. Against loneliness . . . against some inner precipice."

"So you won't come back?"

"I don't know yet, Jackie. Don't wait for me."

Sabina is lying flat on her stomach in the black grass outside the chapel with a book open in front of her.

"All I ask is freedom," she says, and as she looks up at me her pupils dilate despite the bright sunshine, until all that remains of her eyes is black ink and pure pain. "And when freedom is denied me, as it always is, I take it anyway."

I will never forget her eyes, how they widened and shrank in the strong light under the Beckomberga trees. Large, dark and unmoving in her face, hardened by drugs and alcohol. For a long time she was my picture of the future; now I do not know anymore. One evening, as I stand in the window of Ward 6, I see her running down the bank by the birch trees behind Stora Mans with Edvard behind her. By the big oak tree he catches her and pulls her down onto the grass. He snatches off her necklace and pearls fly through the air, cascading like water, blue raindrops.

For months I keep finding pearls in the grass under the oak

tree. Cornflower blue, Indian, cerulean, sky, fading ever more with time; the rain has completely washed away the colour on some of the pearls and they are white as ivory, blanched. At first I intend to give them back, but later there is no-one to give them back to.

⟨⟨⟩⟩

Jim resembles an elderly little boy when he sits in the sunken armchair, making it look enormous, with his long scraggy legs thrust carelessly forward. The armchair is one of the few things that remain after Vita and Henrik; everything else has disappeared, sold long ago when Jim needed money. In the photographs they grow ever younger as the rest of us grow older. Vita was just under forty when she departed, a little younger than I am now, and the light still shines from her eyes in the old black-and-white wedding pictures.

No-one has ever believed Jim would become old. He has always stood beyond the bounds of time and lived according to his own rules, like an overgrown child, dangerous and unruly, and he has always liked death too much for anyone to imagine him in his dotage. I sometimes think Jim managed to avoid all impress of life after adolescence, of ageing; he has always done what he felt like doing, followed all his whims and instincts: dishonesty, deception, drink and desertion. I do not believe he has ever loved anyone. Not me, or my half-brothers, perhaps not even Lone.

23

"Come on, Jackie," he says, oblivious of the fact that he will be seventy next year. "I'll never be old. I've lived too hard for that. And I've never wanted to live. Not really. Not like you."

He has made up his mind to die, again. He announces it, in so many words, as soon as he comes through the door on Jung-frugatan. "I don't want to be old, Jackie. There's nothing left to live for." He has come to Stockholm to say goodbye to Marion and me. In a few months he plans to swim out from the little bay in northern Spain. He has saved a box of Imovane sleeping pills and asked for my blessing; and I have given it to him because I generally give him what he asks for. I have always been silenced by his presence, all thought inside me erased.

"Do as you wish, Jim," I say, briskly. "You always have."

After he left Lone and me for a tiny rented room on Observatoriegatan, Jim began writing to me. That was before he went to Beckomberga.

"Jackie, you must help me, please. Just come for a little while after school, Jackie. You're the only one who can save me now. Won't you come? It's so lonely here."

I never answered his letters because I did not know how to reply, and because I have always had the feeling that I could not rescue Jim even if I tried. In the end he has always been saved by someone else, by a woman like Sabina, or by alcohol.

*

Jim is not himself. His face is pale in spite of the scorching sun over the house in Cariño and he is dressed in a smart suit several sizes too big for him, and elegant shoes, the sort of clothes he would never have worn previously. Before, it was always jeans and washed-out T-shirts and trainers. It looks as though he has dressed up for his own funeral. And the light that has always been in his eyes is there no longer. The beautiful, terrifying, desolate light that spilled over, illuminating the night around him and betraying a special kind of intensity and recklessness, something unstoppable, a raging fire, the sheerest drop. One dark-blue iris is clouded by a faintly milky film, and his glance is restless, searching. Without women and alcohol, without the glimmer of sexual passion for destruction within him, there is nothing left but ash, an old body in a suit too large, without a future, without hope. Like a prancing newt in the air of summer, its tiny elastic body taut, vibrating, glistening with water, bursting with life and energy, then drying up in the winter cold.

Long ago I believed our family was blessed with a special light; I thought no harm could ever befall us. Jim had a way of talking about the world that made me feel we were exalted and chosen, and when I listened to his stories about our life, the world around us brightened. When I came to Beckomberga and met the old men who spoke about themselves like aristocrats and royals, I recognised in them something of Jim. Their lives were also gilded, elevated. They floated alone, slightly above everyone else's lives. Inside themselves they were driving through the world in golden carriages, adored and feared by all.

---

Outside my window the white threads of the winter sun touch the pine trees and turn the treetops into gold before they disappear behind the church of Hedvig Eleonora. For a second I imagine the huge trees on fire. The roots and naked trunks burn like flames in the half-light, but the faint golden glow soon ebbs into shadows. It is an unseasonably warm winter, deceptively mild.

Jim looked frail when we met in Humlegården Park earlier today, unsteady even when sober, disoriented in the new Stockholm. If he has grown old, I can't be young any longer, I thought, as I stood and watched him looking out anxiously for me in the crowds, like a child searching for his parents. Lone is more timeless; sometimes she seems younger than me. I have never heard her speak ill of anyone, not about Jim, nor about anyone else. I think she must have a special aptitude for love. Marion is drawn to her as to a flower.

"Tell me more about Edvard," I say to Jim, who is sitting in the soft circle of lamplight; I have a strong sense that he really is on the way out, that this is our last time together before he finally disappears. He carries on speaking as the light of the blue hour rapidly sinks and is replaced by the cold glare of street lamps.

*

When Edvard and he returned to the hospital at dawn, he was given back his hospital clothes as well as something to help him sleep, a little pale pink tablet. Edvard stopped the car a short distance away and let him get changed under cover of a cluster of pine trees. Jim was let into Ward 43; he crept past the night-shift nurse and lay down to sleep for a while before wake-up time. A few hours later Edvard had resumed his official position behind his desk. Jim and he held long conversations during the therapy sessions, about loneliness and the meaninglessness of everything. Edvard said: "There's no way of knowing whether someone really wants to take his own life." And he continued: "I don't believe you want to die, Jim. You're not a suicide case. I think you were desperate to see your mother again, Vita. I think there was something you wanted to ask her. I want you to make me a promise. For as long as we're making our nightly trips, I want you to cut it out. I need someone like you."

Jim gives me his wide smile as he sits opposite in the velvet armchair and lights a fresh cigarette from the butt end of the old one.

"Edvard always said I wasn't ill. 'You don't really need to be here, Jim,' he said. 'The car will be waiting for you at half ten outside Stora Mans.'"

<hr>

I reach out my hand to Jim to light yet another cigarette. Darkness has fallen around us and his face is lit up by the little flame from the matchstick and then by the glow of the cigarette bobbing through the night.

"Where do you think they are now?"

"Who?"

"The old patients at Beckomberga."

"Here," he says, laughing, "in your armchair."

"What about the others?"

"They're out there, somewhere."

"Yes, but *where* are they?"

"On the streets and in hostels and in prisons, I suppose. Or under bridges. Where else would they be?"

"And you, Jim, where are you?"

"Here at yours, Jackie."

"I know that, but are you happier now?"

"I'll never be happy, but I'm doing well, all the same."

"But why was he admitted to Beckomberga if it wasn't the alcohol?" Lone asks, standing under the stars in her coat, gazing up at Beckomberga's silhouette against the night. She looks young, as she always will, even with grey streaks appearing in her hair, silver strands emerging from her head like moonbeams. It is a dream I have, that Lone will come back with me to the hospital. Here, at the deserted asylum, is where Jim is, and the night; where there is something unfathomable I have always tried to keep at a distance, a brutality and an immense love.

"I don't know," I say. "Why are some people worse at defending themselves?"

Louring sulphurous clouds in the sky above us herald a storm. Sometimes I have the feeling that Lone has not really been touched by life, that after all those years with Jim she has retreated, like a wounded animal.

"What should he be defending himself against?"

"Life, I suppose."

"Ah, that."

Lone gives a short laugh, the soft, ringing laughter that swathes the world in the veils of fables, before she slips out of my thoughts.

# THE NIGHT

*"Male, born 1945, admitted to Beckomberga following suicide attempt . . , within days suffers repeated epileptic seizures as a result of long-term alcohol and prescription drug abuse . . . employment, housing, ex-wife, thirteen-year-old daughter . . . Antabuse treatment started and later discontinued at patient's request . . . suicide risk . . ."*

A sole photograph from Beckomberga: I found it in one of Lone's albums. I have a hat on my head and the old fox-fur boa hanging round my neck. It must have been Edvard who took the photograph on one of her rare visits to Beckomberga, and, strangely, a white butterfly has wandered into the picture and been locked in, sitting forever fixed beside my braid – at first glance you might think it a bow in my hair. There were so many butterflies in those days, and birds; they were everywhere. In the photo we are standing a little apart, as if unaware of the others in the picture, or as if we are just about to go our separate ways. Behind us, scattered clouds are reflected in a window. Lone is moving out of the picture; she has never liked being captured in a photograph. I have bent to pick something off the ground and am covering my hat with my hand so it does not blow away. Jim is the only one standing still, staring straight at the camera with his intense, dark-blue eyes.

Sometimes I think Marion is like Jim; they walk in the same way. Loose, fast, and slightly jerky steps, a sudden joy sweeping through the body like a wind. A current that makes Marion run through life and makes Jim keep on moving, never staying still, never stopping to rest. Marion came to me one stormy night; in the early hours that November morning six years ago I sat in the hospital with a blood-soaked bundle in my arms. He lay wrapped in blankets and blood-stained towels, the room enveloped in a smell of animal and foul water. Out of the bloodstains shone a pair of bright blue eyes, and a heart was beating under the pallid skin that looked several sizes too big. I remember wondering if his eyes had gleamed like that in the darkness inside me.

When Jim comes he jokes with Marion for a few minutes and then forgets he is here. Marion's light voice eludes him, as if children exist in a frequency to which Jim is not attuned. Marion likes it when he is here, nonetheless; he looks at him with delight in his eyes and asks when he is coming back to us.

"I don't know," Jim answers. "Maybe I'll never come back."

"Why won't you come back?"

"Because life is hard and living just gets harder with time. You should be glad you don't know what's in store for you, Inspector Belmondo."

Just before I fall asleep I can smell smoke. I search through the apartment, ashtrays, the gas oven, old burnt-out candles, but nothing is on fire and I have learned to sleep regardless. Just below the surface of my consciousness is a trail of purple smoke and at night comes terror: a cold band around my chest, a liquid chill running down my spine, seeping through my veins, like snow, like dry ice. I wake again in the night and imagine that the earth is about to collide with a star; I wake because I am falling. I am afraid that the block of flats will topple over, I am afraid that everything will be gone when I rise, I am afraid of the slow advance of wars across the world. It is our long night, Jim's and mine, opening up beneath me like the dark vault of heaven; and I go in to Marion and look at him, spreadeagled like a little cross on the bed, his hair dark with perspiration. I wish I could protect him against the night, against my face and my gaze; I wish I could carry him still, inside me.

∽∾∽

On the ends of tree branches in Clock-House Park hang large transparent drops that shatter when they lose their grip on the bark and fall to the ground, wasted, destroyed. Within each droplet is a mirror and in each mirror a solitary world: patients who walk amidst the crashing of waves along the beach below Sankta Maria; unmarked graves at the edge of the hospital grounds and the dead from so-called Lunatics' Castle, without kith or kin, floating in cement tanks filled with formaldehyde before ending up on the dissecting tables of medical students; Jim in the ambulance on its way over the bridges to Beckomberga; and Sabina dancing backwards through the dim light of Ward 6 in a faded petticoat. And it is not painful: it is simply that the situation has a special clarity about it. The pattern in the tree trunks outside the window is as clear to me as if I were holding a magnifying glass in my hand.

"Did you really want to leave all this, Jim?" I ask. "I mean, die. Did you really want to do that?"

"I suppose I did. I thought there wasn't anything left."

"But . . ."

"Jackie, it's not as bad as all that. Sometimes there just isn't anything left."

"Don't you want to come home?"

"I'm already home."

On visits later in the spring of my fourteenth birthday, Jim holds court on the small bank under the birch trees outside Stora Mans. The first white butterflies zigzag between tall blades of grass and from far away we hear him telling stories and singing outside the little ward by the birch trees, surrounded by staff, patients and relatives. We approach slowly under the droop of leafy coronets, Lone still in coat and boots despite the summer warmth, while birds shriek crazily in the trees, their long cries dark with torment. Jim has always hovered over the abyss with a smile, drunken and invincible, always making people laugh. It is his gift to us.

It must have been night when they brought him here. He had been found in the snow by the motorway heading to the airport, and after his stomach had been pumped at Sabbatsberg Hospital he was taken to Beckomberga. A few hours earlier he had checked into a hotel in Norrtull, where he had swallowed all his sleeping tablets and helped them down with a bottle of brandy. Then he walked out onto the motorway in the direction of the airport with the aim of catching an aeroplane somewhere, anywhere at all, Paris, St Petersburg, Moscow, and by the time he reached his destination he would be dead. But he never got that far. A few hundred metres from the hotel he fell down asleep in a snowdrift.

Before me I see birds of prey waiting by Jim's lifeless body at the side of the road and the last of the sky above as it slowly disappears between the black tops of the pine trees. In the distance the sound of sirens, of footsteps in clogs, keys, doors slamming behind Jim as he is rushed down brightly lit corridors; and then the immense blackness surging out of the old blood-red hospital building on Beckomberga Avenue outside Stockholm.

And it must be I who asked, long ago, in another age, when we were still standing under the leafy birch trees outside Stora Mans.

"Jimmie?"

"Yes?"

"Wasn't there anything to keep you in this world that time?"

"What might that have been?"

"I don't know . . . me, maybe . . ."

"Remember this, Jackie," Jim said, laughing. "The stuff that makes other people happy has never made me happy. And you have always been free. You've never needed a dad and you'll never need a husband."

—∞—

He was lying asleep on the grass outside the Royal Library with several empty bottles beside him. A German Shepherd I had never seen before was sitting next to him. At first I thought he was dead, he was sleeping so deeply. I crouched down beside him and after a while I could see a faint pulse in his neck, as if a tiny lizard were trapped inside the fragile skin. I was scared the dog would attack me, but it sat absolutely still, as if it had not noticed I was there. A book lay open near the bottles and my eyes fell on some of its lines. *What damages a human being is sin. The light of eternity will finally be extinguished. Love is unnatural.* The dog was still sitting quite motionless, surveying the park. Perhaps I should have woken Jim, but I did not dare, so I sat down on a park bench some distance away and waited. I stayed there until it grew dark. After a few hours he stood up and looked around; he picked up his bottles and newspapers and sauntered off. He walked past so close to me, as I sat on the bench, that I could smell him, but he did not see me. It was the last time I saw him before he was admitted to hospital.

# THE LAST PATIENT
## (STILL IN THE LIGHT)

One conversation with the consultant on the top floor remains before it is time to leave. Dr Janowski is already on his way, his surgery packed up into boxes. By now his thoughts are in his new room on the island of Kungsholmen, on a level with the birds, where he will have a view right over to City Hall. Olof sits clutching his suitcase and looking out of the window. He has few possessions: wallet, reading glasses, medicines, pyjamas, suit, and an encyclopaedia that the consultant Harald Rabe gave him long ago. On the floor beside him he has a globe. His cardigan is missing some buttons and is several sizes too small, and his old-man hands rest on his knees.

"I was afraid you wouldn't come," he says.

"We'd agreed the time."

"Yes. I . . . The clock's stopped out there at half-past three. It's the time in the night most people die. Though Dad died in the afternoon. Two o'clock. I found out the day after."

"I remember, Olof. You were sad."

"Yes."

"You got into fights."

"Yes."

"And then you stopped."

Olof gazes at him wide-eyed.

"Do you think I'll be alright out there?"

"Yes, I do."

"Do you really?"

"Yes, I have high hopes for you. Always have had. You know that."

"You said you were my hope when I didn't have any hope myself."

"Yes, and I have been. Now you must bear that hope yourself, Olof."

"I'd rather stay here."

"Why would you want to do that?"

"My friends are here."

"Olof . . ."

"But I have no other friends. And you're my friend, Dr Janowski. You said you're my friend."

"I am your friend, but that doesn't mean we're going to see each other again. You're going to have real friends out there."

Olof stares out of the window again, his eyes glistening.

"I don't think so, but it will be nice to be able to pick flowers whenever I want to. I'll go to Haga Park and Gärdet and Lill-Jansskogen."

"And what else?"

"I might win the jackpot in the lottery."

STORA MANS,
MARCH 1986

Clock-House Park is deserted. Muffled voices can be heard outside the examination room, people moving about in the corridor. The shirt Jim is wearing is the colour of cigarettes, the remnants of old sunshine lingering on it, and he sits opposite Edvard in the room next to the hospital clock. It is like sitting inside a giant body, a heart of iron that is working away right beside him, an alien, menacing pulse. Every morning, a great despondency in his chest that stretches out like a wasteland. A blazing sun within him, his blood screaming for the warmed brandy running through his veins. From the records: *Well-groomed, expression rather haggard. Has been highly strung and nervous all his life.*

Edvard's eyes seem to have been lit up from within by a darting, insistent brightness, a light that makes Jim feel defenceless, as if it were passing through his skin like an x-ray, illuminating everything, his ribcage and inside it his heart, suspended like a shadow.

"What's the ideology behind all of this?"

Jim returns to that question; every day he climbs the many steps up to Edvard to ask about the ideas behind the hospital, the principal theories.

"There is no ideology, Jim. Let it go now."

Edvard takes off his spectacles and leaves them on the desk, where the sun shines through them. The desk is cluttered with piles of papers and old books left open, as if he were reading them all at the same time. His hands are pale, slightly freckled.

"So you have a daughter?"

"Yes."

He puts his glasses back on for a moment. Rimless, only the thin lens protecting his eyes.

"When you were admitted you said you had no children."

"Did I?"

"Yes. I asked you."

Jim looks out of the window. A milky white sky, fiery yellow streaks.

"It felt as though I had no children. It felt as though everything had gone."

"And now?"

"Now I don't know."

We wait for Jim in one of the corridors. The walls are green like the inside of a pool, and a square of light comes out of every room. The sound of voices in the distance, a solitary black fly crawling along the wall. A nurse comes towards us in white clogs and her fair hair hangs in a plait down her back. Inger Vogel is the name on her badge. She tells us to wait, Jim will soon be ready for us. When he eventually appears in a shirt and a pair of baggy trousers I have never seen before, Lone gets to her feet.

"Hello, Jim."

He stares at us as if we were risen from the dead. Round his waist is a gold belt that looks like a curtain tie-back.

"You came."

"Yes," Lone says softly.

"I thought I'd never see you again."

Lone hands him a bag of clothes that we have collected from the woman on Observatoriegatan.

"Anne was wondering where you got to. I didn't know what to say. She wonders whether you're going to carry on renting the room. You should have rung us."

"I didn't know where you were."

"We were in Morocco," I say.

"I knew where you were, but I didn't have a number. I didn't think you'd come back."

We should never have left Jim alone with the winter and the snow that kept on falling on the city while we were away, but Lone wants to be on her own now. And for the first time she can afford to travel, because Jim is no longer spending all our money.

"What do you do all day?" I ask.

"Rest. Play chess. Talk to a doctor. And there's a girl here I like. Sabina."

Lone has gone out to stretch her legs in the corridor. I sit at the foot of his bed. Right on the edge with my feet touching the floor. A medicine trolley rattles past outside. Inger Vogel goes

47

in and out of the rooms with a tray of small plastic medicine cups. A slight, angelic figure in clogs. Jim knocks the contents of his cup back and returns it to the tray.

"Can't you go out?" I ask, gazing at the clouds drifting past outside. Small broken clouds, blurred at the edges. A fine wire mesh runs through the glass in the window like a spider's web. At first you do not see it, but then you do; the pane cannot be broken from the inside.

"I can go out sometimes."

"Can you go out on your own?"

"No."

I look at him and he looks away. His eyes dark blue, like mine. In the distance the drumming sound of heavy rain approaching, the sky's watery grey membrane criss-crossed by grainy black lines.

"Did you really think we wouldn't come back?"

"No."

"Lone might change her mind."

"I don't think she will. I wouldn't if I were her."

"Come back?"

"I wouldn't love me. I can understand why she doesn't."

A few days earlier Jim telephoned to say he is ill. Lone and I have just arrived from the airport and are standing outside the front door when we hear the telephone ringing in the apartment. I rush through the bright rooms and snatch up the receiver and Jim's voice enters my head. Outside the window the snow is falling and I think it must have changed his voice, because he sounds as though he were a long way down under the ground. Or maybe it is just that the telephone wires are weighed down by the snow. As we speak it sounds as though he is cold, and I think of the warm golden sea where I have been swimming for the last few weeks, looking for shells and starfish; I can still feel the throb of the ocean within me, rising and falling with the waves, wanting to pull me out into the deep, where I could have floated forever.

Now and then during the conversation, which mostly consists of silences, I hear the sound of a coin rattling down a slot. "Is it snowing where you are?" I ask in the end.

"I don't know," Jim says. "I'm standing in a corridor and there aren't any windows, but it hasn't stopped snowing since you went."

"What sort of illness have you got?" I ask into the warm mouth of the receiver.

"My wings have grown too big and I can't fly anymore."

"What does that mean?"

"I don't know really," Jim says. "I'll ask the doctor when he comes, but I'll probably be here a while."

"Where are you then?"

"At Beckomberga. Do you know what that is?"

"Yes, I think so," I say, as something cold inside me brushes against my ribs.

"May I speak to Lone?"

"Yes."

I hold the receiver to my heart for a long time before I hand it to Lone, who is standing in front of me with her coat over her arm, and I watch her face as she talks. She has opened the window so that an icy draught streams into the room and I am cold in my quilted jacket. After a while I notice that little puddles of water have formed around my snowy boots. Lone holds the receiver pressed hard against her ear and while she listens she gazes out of the window with a strangely vacant smile.

Lone had been lying for days on end on a kilim at the top of the beach next to the tall grass where it met the dry, cracked asphalt. She was deep in her books, and when she fell asleep in the heat the wind turned the pages for a while before moving on over the beach. Stray dogs, hungry and thin, would prowl the water's edge on the lookout for fish and rubbish washed ashore. The nights were starlit; one morning a black kitten floated onto the beach. Often, I sat on the balcony, looking at the pitch-dark mountains in the distance and thinking we could stay here forever, lie dozing under the ceiling fan and listen to the daybreak calls of minarets. Had Jim been with us, everything would have been different.

The stones in the sand that were laid bare when the waves drew back were like the birthmarks on Lone's back; it looked as though someone had shaken a brush dipped in black paint over her shoulders. A mark for every year that passed, as if a black sun were shining over her body. She sat on the balcony until her face turned brown and her skin grew deceptively smooth and soft. I had almost no blemishes on my body, just a sprinkling of freckles here and there. I did not resemble her in any way. When I looked at myself in the mirror, it was his face I saw, Jim's. The narrow, dark-blue eyes, the fickleness, the void.

---

A few months earlier we had walked along Kammakargatan, through Tegnérlunden Park and further on to Observatoriegatan, where Jim was now going to live. Lone had asked Jim to move out. The mist wafted around us, the trees stood almost bare in Spökparken, the "haunted park", and I held Lone's hand in mine. We accompanied Jim, with his suitcase, to the small room on Observatoriegatan. He stood in the doorway and looked at us when we were about to take our leave. He and Lone had shared a farewell drink together, rum as black as gall. He stood like a shadow against the door frame.

"Don't go, Lone. Don't leave me. I won't be able to do this."

But we did go. We walked down Drottninggatan, the Christmas lights twinkling above us with a thousand stars.

When I arrived at Observatoriegatan after school to visit him, he was lying on the bed-settee with the blinds down. A subdued light filtered across the room and he had forgotten everything. When he looked at me he saw nothing.

"What have you done with your beautiful mother? Have you lost her like I did?"

It was as if he had forgotten that light existed. He no longer turned the lamps on and the blinds were always drawn. Lone had been the light of his life and now she was gone. I sat beside him and watched the sun disappear, it went so fast; one minute there was sunshine over the city, a light in its heart, and the next it was black, like being in a sack.

After Jim moves out, he still regularly comes back with a little carrier bag to sleep over. In the mornings, when Lone and I hurry off in the darkness, we leave him lying in the double bed. There is a smell around him in the sheets of something neglected, a hint of earth and dereliction, of loneliness. After a month or two he stops coming back, and when I ring him on Observatoriegatan he does not answer.

He rests his head against her coat and she strokes his hair; it is coarse and unwashed, the smell unfamiliar, a faint trace of medicine and institution, the dull, stale, white odour of festering bandages, mortuary, soap.

"I have to go now," Lone says gently.

Finally, Jim looks at her. His eyes are pale blue in the dim light.

"Stay with me, my love."

"I can't stay."

"Just for a little while. Sit with me."

"I really have to go."

"Why did you come then?"

"Because you asked me to."

"So you didn't come for me?"

"I don't know, Jim. I came because you needed me."

"But not like that? Not for me?"

"What does it matter? I came, didn't I? No-one else has. There's only been me. And Jackie."

Suddenly a white bird flies past in the corridor outside. An ocean bird or maybe some sort of bird of prey. It is huge and white and shining brightly and makes me think of the future. When I run out into the hallway I see it disappear up the stairwell further along.

On the bus home after our first visits to Beckomberga, Lone and I looked at each other as if we had just woken up from a long, bewildering dream. Her strawberry-blonde hair was in a mess and the lifeless industrial landscape rushed past outside. I do not think we ever talked about these visits after that first telephone call from Jim. We took the bus there, sat for a few hours in the ward, then took the bus back to the city. Kammakargatan was in shadows when we returned, a cold white sun

53

low in the sky, and Lone lay down on the sofa with a book. When spring came and she no longer wanted to visit, I started going there on my own. Lone never tried to stop me doing what I wanted to do. I have always had the freedom I needed.

# THE MAP
# (THE ARCHITECTURE
# OF SORROW)

A narrow dove-grey stretch of road, carrying the occasional car, goes past Bromma Church and the cluster of houses beside it. A small shop and a school. Beyond these, wide open fields and forest. An avenue of lime trees leads up to the main hospital buildings, which enclose a rectangular courtyard. The Clock-House, or Administration, is the heart of the place; beside it stand two enormous hospital wings, Stora Mans for men and Stora Kvinns for women. Opposite them is the kitchen block. A beautiful park which surrounds the hospital is encircled by a fence several metres high; entry to the buildings means passing through Security at the north or south gatehouse. Neatly trimmed whitebeam trees, rose bushes and saplings from the other side of the world; gatehouses and walls; everything in strict symmetry. Dispersed across the grounds are solitary confinement units and housing for the staff. The two largest pavilions can accommodate over four hundred patients, some in single rooms and the rest in supervised dormitories of eight to ten beds.

The architect Carl E. Westman is the man behind what is eventually to become one of Europe's largest psychiatric hospitals. On his sprawling drawing boards at the Medical Council, sketches evolve of a small town on the outskirts of the city, which will contain all that someone out of the ordinary needs.

As the rays of a hazy evening sun fall on them, his finely pencilled lines slowly grow into the buildings he has envisioned. He has resolved that the front of Beckomberga will be of a subdued shade, a rust-red that looks like the colour of clotted blood or the faint light of dusk, its position such that it will always be sunlit.

By early summer 1927 the city has bought the Beckomberga area called Lilla Ängby from the tobacco magnate Knut Ljunglöf, and in the spring of 1929 work begins to the west of Stockholm. The land consists chiefly of woods and areas that have been clear-felled; nearby is a small lake, Kyrksjön, and the stagnant brown water of Lake Judarn. During the summer of 1931 the skeleton of Beckomberga Hospital starts to emerge out of the earth.

In the course of his time at the Medical Council, Carl E. Westman will design and build three mental hospitals: Sankta Maria in Helsingborg, Beckomberga in Stockholm, and Umedalen in Umeå. Excepting the sea, which always pounds the shore next to Sankta Maria, and its roar and the smell of salt and the ever-present seabirds, the hospitals are similar: a few structures along the edge of an elongated courtyard, like a barracks. Plain, discreetly coloured façades with steep, usually hipped, roofs. Bars secure the windows, but Westman has made them look natural, part of the style, and it takes a while before one notices them from the outside. The guiding architectural principles are economy, austerity, starkness and simplicity; the design is not intended to arouse expectations the institution cannot fulfil. It is monumental yet unpretentious, grand yet sombre. Its interior has wide corridors which open onto dormitories and day rooms to facilitate surveillance. Room after room in verdigris green, with the view out of the many windows the same from every angle. The building opposite all but blocks the sky, sparing only streaks of birds and light and the barracks yard below, a place with no shadows and no sanctuary where nothing can escape the buildings' countless eyes. I am struck by how overwhelming the huge edifices must have appeared to the patients and their visitors before the trees and bushes grew to their full size.

In Jim's time the area around the hospital was not particularly built-up; beyond the fence was primarily woodland and field. The sick have always been kept at a distance, away from the city community, and a circle of desolation has often surrounded large mental hospitals; but over time the city has edged closer. Some years after the hospital opened, the residential area of Norra Ängby was created just a stone's throw from the south gatehouse, and soon rows of terraced houses and shops jostled side by side with hospital buildings. In the first half of the '30s, when Bromma Airport was built close to Beckomberga, aircraft climbing and descending became a feature of the view from the hospital, an image of freedom appearing and promptly vanishing.

From the turn of the last century the number of people admitted to psychiatric hospitals increased. Accordingly, the Medical Council built a raft of new hospitals in Sweden: Beckomberga and Långbro in Stockholm, Sankta Maria in Helsingborg, Lillhagen in Gothenburg, St Olof in Visby, Umedalen, Sidsjön, Säter, St Gertrud, Sundby and Konradsberg – affectionately known as Lunatics' Castle. Some argue that the increase in mental illness is simply evidence of the state's control over citizens, and that its diagnosis is no more than a hypothesis to explain undesirable behaviour. Others say migration from rural areas into the city made it harder over this time for the ill to live outside institutions, and correlate the difficulty with the surge in cases of syphilis and dementia. In the city the mentally ill were more vulnerable and isolated. In any event, the definition of what at the time was termed insanity must have widened. At the end of 1900 there were 4,400 people in large mental hospitals. Fifty years later the number was almost 33,000.

Inscribed in letters of graphite gold spanning the entrance is an account of events, above the unseeing visage of the façade, with its arms, with its laws:

> By agreement between the state and the city of Stockholm in the year 1925 the city assumed the care of its

mentally ill. To which end the City Council in the year 1929 ruled that Beckomberga Hospital be built and in 1932–1933 this hospital was opened.

There is something utopian about this period, and within the gilt inscription lie all the hopes that were once linked to the new hospital – this magnificent, imposing welfare edifice. The sick of the city would have a new home where they would want for nothing; someone would at last look after the unfortunates who "had met with insanity". The dream can be glimpsed in the golden words of hope – it still exists – of a different kind of hospital, a new world in which no-one will be excluded, where order and nurture will prevail, where the human detritus that no-one knows what to do with – the useless and the unwanted who have lived for centuries in cages underground – will be brought up into the light to be washed and clothed in hospital stripes.

It is easy to idealise the institution as the perfect place that will do everything we human beings cannot bring ourselves to do for one another. And yet it is terrifying too, because it represents the imperfect in us: failure, weakness, loneliness.

# THE LAST PATIENT
## (STILL IN THE LIGHT)

As Dr Janowski turns the pages of his medical records, Olof twists his hands. Enormous hands that look as though they belong to a stronger man.

"You can ask whatever you want, Olof."

"How long have I been here?"

"You've been here for sixty-three years. You came here for the first time in 1932. In the autumn."

A cautious smile spreads across his face.

"That's an awfully long time."

"Yes. You're old now."

"I remember dancing in the assembly hall on New Year's Eve, 1954. Jussi Björling sang for us that night. Hanna Johansson was her name, and she was dancing without her nurse's uniform on, without her shoes, without her glasses. We stayed in the chapel till dawn. Jussi Björling had been discharged the previous spring and he came back to sing for us. Hanna Johansson finished in 1971."

"That was before my time. I wish I'd been around that night."

The smile swiftly leaves Olof's face and he lowers his voice.

"What's out there now?"

"A whole new world. You know you have to watch out for cars, you can't just step straight out into the road."

He looks down at the large hands on his knee.

"Do you know that Mum sometimes comes to me in a dream? She only comes in a dream, nowhere else. Why does God send me dreams like that?"

"Why do you think God sends you dreams like that?"

"I don't know, but when the end of the world is here, Mum will come back to me."

"Do you really believe that?"

Olof gives another tentative smile, a pale light suffusing his face.

"Yes. I'm always waiting for a miracle. A divine intervention."

He raises his hands and draws a careful outline in the air as he continues to speak.

"I've tried to sketch out the hospital, but it's difficult. I don't actually know what it looks like on the outside. I don't know how the buildings are connected. I've got these windows here and the exercise yard here and the path to the chapel. I know it's bigger, but I wouldn't be able to do a sketch that matches reality."

"What do you think reality is like?"

"That's what I have to find out. But I'm scared."

"What are you scared of?"

"That they won't like me out there."

# THE LANDSCAPE

Rivulets of water are streaming through the Beckomberga woods, everything is awash in the flooding after the dazzling spring rains. Edvard stands at the window, surveying the park. There is no-one there; a gentle breeze touches the treetops, as if an invisible hand were stroking them. All the patients are sitting in the dining room, apart from Jim, who stayed behind at the end of discussion time.

"I want to go home."

"And what do you think it would be like at home?"

"I don't know. I haven't thought about it. You carry your misfortune with you wherever you go."

"You can't go home to Lone anymore."

"I know."

"Where would you live?"

"I don't know. At a hotel. For a while. Temporarily."

"And then what?"

"And then what? I don't know. I'd start drinking again."

"And what would that be like, do you think?"

Jim smiles broadly.

"Do you want to know what I think?"

"Yes."

"I think it would be wonderful. Before I came here I'd decided to drink myself to death. I thought it would be quick."

*

In the afternoon he follows Inger Vogel to the medicine room. He loves being there; without the pills that are stored in it his soul would be extinguished. As soon as they are inside, she steps out of her clogs and pulls her white uniform up to her hips.

"Open the cupboard," he whispers, loosening her hair from the heavy bun on the back of her head.

"Why should I open the cupboard?"

"Because you love me, because you want the best for me, because you know what real love is."

The smell of starch from her uniform mingles with the smell of camphor and morphine as they stand there, charged with electricity, with desire and abstinence, and all the time Inger Vogel has one hand on the door handle – to be able to feel the vibration of a key in the lock.

"Do I?"

"Yes, just now you do."

As if in a trance she unlocks the cupboard and brings out the little vial of brown liquid that resembles a solar eclipse, and when at last the drug is in his bloodstream and reaches his nervous system, something inside him splays open like a fan. Brightness and intensity, and a faint, sunny ripple under his skin. Inger Vogel's sultry, dappled eyes grow bluer and deeper and suddenly the skin on her neck and under her arms, which had just that moment felt dull and slack beneath his hands, is supple and alive.

"You're so beautiful, Inger," he whispers, "so incredibly beautiful."

Vita is standing over by the window. Her face is in shadow, the light at her back. He is the only person in the world awake as the first light of dawn filters in through the blind. The sun always returns to him, whatever may have happened during the night. Vita has on the same old dress as before, the pale blue silk one with mother-of-pearl.

"Jimmie. I've changed my mind. I want to come back to you."

Jim pulls the blanket tighter around his body.

"It's not possible, Vita. Surely you must have known that when you went? Otherwise you wouldn't have gone."

She turns away from him and opens a gap in the blind, letting a strip of light pour into the room.

"But I didn't want to die. I only wanted to disappear for a while."

"A while?"

"Yes. I didn't understand what eternity was."

"And now you know."

"I didn't know what it would be like without you."

Jim pulls the cover over his head and hides his face in the warm darkness.

"I don't think he'll be coming down today," Lone says, snapping the book shut and standing up.

"Why won't he?"

"Maybe he needs to be on his own."

On the streets, people are walking around in tears. There is a strange mood on the underground; at the scene of the murder there are mounds of winter roses. It is not only Jim who feels the loss of Olof Palme.

"I don't think he can see us just now. I don't think he can see anyone."

"Not you, maybe," I say, and sit down again.

Lone is someone else when she is reading; she loses herself for hours, she mellows. From a distance it looks as though a huge butterfly has landed on her lap. Once we went to a butterfly house in Vienna; massive azure-blue butterflies fluttered through the air like giant eyes, drawn to her pretty red coat, as if impelled by her beauty, by something precious within her. She waved her handbag at the enormous gold and purple butterflies, and Jim and I laughed at her. All we wanted was a butterfly's caress with its satiny wing, but that would never happen to us. I look up at the window in Ward 43, the sightless silvery eye. There is no-one there.

Walking through the grove of birch trees comes a group of old women. They appear to be lost, stopping now and then to look up at the treetops. A woman shakes one of the birches, and for a moment they are standing in golden rain.

"Why do you always wear that hat when we're here?"

"Don't you like it?"

"Yes. But you can't see your beautiful face."

The hat shades my face and hides my eyes; with the hat on my head I feel protected. I got it from the man who asks if I want any sweets whenever I am in his airless shop, where the light is always dim. Inside the shop on Drottninggatan time seems to have stood still, and the old things he sells have nothing to do with the world outside. There are seldom any customers, and if any do stumble in they hurry out again because they sense his unwillingness to part with the feathers and the hats and the stuffed animals. I like to wander around amongst the foxes and the birds, their amber eyes unmoving, and walk between the colossal china Dalmatians. Sometimes he lets me choose something from his collection. "What is it you're actually looking for, my little sparrow?" Usually I decline haughtily, but I cannot resist the hat, even though it is moth-eaten and smells of misfortune.

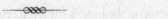

Jim is white-faced and the palms of his hands are cold and wet when I touch them; he is sitting cross-legged on last year's grass, without a coat.

"They got him in the end," he says over and over again, crying, his mouth open. "I knew all along they'd get him."

We have waited for hours, and finally he has come out to see us and has sat down on the grass. I understand how sad he is, the whole world is grieving now, but it makes me uneasy when he does not stop weeping. After all, there is nothing we can do.

"You'll get cold," Lone says, offering him her hand. "Come and sit next to us."

I go off for a walk round the park. In the middle is a chapel; my hand is pale against the green façade and through the open door I can hear faint music. Inside the chapel it is absolutely still; particles of dust float in the air, a girl on her own in a spotted skirt is lying on the floor, looking up at the ceiling, a lit cigarette between her fingers. Murals on the ceiling show distorted, chubby angels wrestling with each other. On the floor a narrow strip of sunlight meets the girl in the skirt, making her seem lit up from within. For a long time I stand looking at her. Every so often she raises her hand, as if to point at one of the angels, but then lets it drop to the floor. When I come out, someone has lowered the flag to half mast.

Jim is lying on the bench, his head resting on Lone's lap, and he looks up at her.

"I'll get over it, won't I, Lone? We'll all get over it."

He laughs at the sun.

"It's not me who's dead. And not you either. It just feels strange because I'm here. As if the world out there is collapsing too."

—ᘒᘒᘒ—

After the last lesson at school I go into Tegnérlunden Park to smoke a quick cigarette. I sit in the warmth of the first spring sun. A pair of pink pants and a fox fur boa are dangling from one of the smaller trees, where they have been hanging for days. When I shake the tree the boa falls onto the snow. I try to reach the knickers with a stick, but they are too high.

An old woman has taken a seat on a bench not far away. Perhaps those are her things that have ended up in the tree.

"Are they your things?" I shout.

She is sitting in a strangely bent position, as if about to fall off the bench, and does not reply. When I come closer I see it is not a woman at all, only a fur coat that has been left behind on the bench. I pick it up and hold it against my cheek. It is silky smooth and cold as the snow, and has a silver lining. It gives off a strong smell of moths and cigarette smoke.

I look in at the shop and let the man admire it. I feel like a fabulous animal as his hands caress it. I do not show him the boa because I have a feeling that I have seen it in his shop before.

"That cat is worth a fortune. If you get tired of it, I'll gladly buy it off you."

From that moment I wear it all the time. I keep it on during lessons in school and when I visit the hospital. Every afternoon I hide it in the cellar before I go up to Lone.

*

"I'm going now, Mum," I call into the gloomy apartment. I am standing in the hall with my shoes on and the fox fur boa wrapped round my neck, staring at my reflection. In the mirror I look older than I am; my eyes have darkened and my face is thinner; my mouth looks as though it belongs to a different girl. Lone comes out, kisses my cheek, and straightens my hat. She is never sentimental; by the time I am out of the door she has returned to her books, and when I come back she is still sitting in the same place by the kitchen table, reading.

The old men are standing in the sun, their cigarettes lit, waiting for nothing. Humble in the face of their situation, they gaze up at the clouds and aeroplanes passing low over the hospital. They rarely complain, they never oppose hospital rules, they are unprotesting even if, after minor infractions, Edvard and Inger Vogel decide they must be carted away. At first I think they talk about everything, as if they have no secrets, but after a while I realise they are always telling the same stories, two or three anecdotes that they constantly repeat. Alcohol is the reason many of them are here, sometimes amphetamines or morphine. Nostalgia is not a luxury they can afford, they never miss anyone who has disappeared; it takes no more than an instant for them to forget those who have left after being discharged – the departed are a reminder of lives already lost.

The old men of Stora Mans seldom receive visitors. Most have been in so long there is probably no-one outside who still remembers them. The occasional woman – a girlfriend or a mother – visits the younger men, bearing chocolate cakes and newspapers. Some of the women bring needlework with which they busy themselves during visiting time.

A girl stands at the door, looking at us; it is the girl from the chapel. She is wearing one of the hospital gowns, her legs bare underneath. I catch a glimpse of a lace nightdress beneath the gown, and a shiny blue pearl necklace. Right at the bottom, a pair of men's brown slippers. Later I will recognise her by her shuffling, Sabina's special way of shuffling. When I look up she is watching us with something akin to a smile. Jim wakes from his stupor when she comes into the room, he lights up as if someone has switched on a lamp inside him.

"Sabina, come and say hello to Jackie."

"Hello, Jackie. I love your fur coat."

She takes my hand in hers, which is moist and limp. She is thirty-six, as I will later learn, but she is like a child, or a teen-ager. She has smudges of mascara under her eyes, as if she has just been crying or sleeping too long. Her hair is streaked and matted and she appears to have gone out in her underclothes. I find out that she grew up at the Natural History Museum; her father is a curator there. She boasts of having a burial place at Hedvig Eleonora Church: all curators and their families have.

"Congratulations," says Jim. "The rest of us are happy when

we find an apartment. What use will this grave be to you?"

"I didn't say I was happy. But Dad came here to the ward once with a stuffed falcon instead of flowers. Then I was happy. I think they threw it out afterwards."

Jim smiles.

"Are you allowed out in the exercise yard?"

"I'm not allowed anything anymore. Before, they let me go to the swimming baths. Now they think I'm going to swim away."

She gives a harsh laugh. Jim takes her hand.

"Why are you here, Sabina?"

"I harmed myself. What about you?"

"I fell."

She touches his cheek with her hand.

"Oh, sweetheart. Did it hurt?"

Jim laughs.

"It doesn't hurt as much now. I like being here since I met you."

She sits on the edge of the bed for a while and looks at me with her big eyes before getting up to leave.

"She could have anything she wanted," Jim says to me, as she stands in the doorway with her back to us.

She turns.

"I heard that. Hypotheses really don't help me at all."

After she has gone Jim falls asleep. I see Sabina pass a few times in the corridor outside, before I nod off beside him.

The bed beside Jim's is always empty. There it stands, made up, white, as if awaiting someone. We each lie on a bed, looking up at the ceiling, I in my fur and he in baggy trousers that belong to the hospital. We play chess to pass the time, and when he is asleep I read the books on his bedside table. *A Time on Earth. All the World Balloon Mad.*

I look at him while he sleeps and think that I cannot leave him here. When he opens his eyes they are black and full of tears.

"I ruined the forests," he whispers.

"Did you?"

"Yes."

Then he rolls over and goes back to sleep.

I find a channel on the television in the dayroom and on the news it appears that the world does still exist, it is just that we have ended up outside it.

"Can't you see the trees, how they've changed?" I say when he wakens.

"Which trees?"

"The ones outside here. It's spring now."

"No, I've not seen them."

He is pleased I have come, he says, and yet he is so tired he keeps falling asleep every few minutes while we are talking, and when he wakes up he looks at me as if he has never seen my face before.

"What have you done with your hat?"

I point to where it is lying in the sun on the chair by the door.

"There it is. I thought it was a little cake waiting there for us. Where did you go earlier on?"

"I've just been sitting here, watching you," I say.

"I thought you were dead."

"We were only on holiday."

I sit there for a while every day before I set off down the stairs and walk out of the hospital grounds to the bus. Jim watches me from the window. He has never looked at me before as he does here; now I am all he has in the world and the world is this hospital with its fence and its locked doors, and behind the wire mesh he raises his hand in farewell.

"Come back to me," he whispers.

The little telephone kiosk is steaming up with our breath. When Jim has replaced the receiver he looks at me for a long time without saying anything. His eyes are dark: like coal, like graphite, like spilt ink.

"Who was it?" I finally ask.

"It was Vita."

"Isn't she dead?"

"I thought she was too, but she just rang."

"Did she ring here?"

"Yes."

"How did she know we were here?"

"I don't know. She didn't say."

"Okay. So what did she say?"

"She said that she was sorry she never got to meet you. She asked me which arrow flies forever."

"Which is it?"

"I don't know. That's what I don't know," he says, weeping. His tears fall onto the smooth stone floor. He lifts up the receiver again to make another call. It emits a muffled tone, a song, or a distant ocean.

"You mustn't be afraid of me, Jackie."

"I'm not afraid of you."

Inger Vogel is standing at the door, blocking the light. She looks as though she has been there for a while.

"Time to run along home now, love."

Jim is playing the piano again in the dayroom. He is playing without sheet music, hard and fast and by sheer instinct. Deep inside the music he has no need to confront the world outside, a world in which music is all he has dreamt about. From a distance it looks as though he is trying to smash the keys.

"What have you ruined now?" I ask when he eventually lets his hands sink back down to his knees.

An elderly man is sitting a short distance away, looking at us attentively. I stare at him until he shifts his gaze. From the corner of my eye I see him gently rest his head in his hands.

"I'm too sad to talk about it," Jim says.

"Talk about something else then."

He is silent for a moment, and he fiddles with the gold sash that he now wears over his pyjamas, as if he were royalty.

"I have nightmares. I dream that God has come to fetch me."

Jim has never mentioned God before, and I think that he must now feel terribly alone.

"Where does he want to take you?"

He lifts his hands and retreats into the music again. The old man is still there, his head resting on the table, as if in prayer, his little jacket pulled tight across his back. It makes me think of a picture Sabina showed me, a photograph from behind of a naked woman lying on a floor in prayer.


On my way out into the corridor Edvard's huge hand falls between my shoulder blades, as if he were taking a discreet measurement of my back. I turn around and he drops his hand. I have only seen him from a distance before, when he has been rushing past further down the corridor, his white coat open; he has never noticed me. Now he looks at me with a big smile.

"So, you're the daughter then?"

"Yes, I am."

"What a little treasure. We'll have to be careful with you."

"I don't know about that," I say, mainly because I do not want silences. We are the only ones in the corridor.

"I think so. You're like Jimmie. You have the same eyes, the same way of occupying a room. Proprietorial."

I raise my eyelids without thinking. Edvard laughs and pushes me away as if I were a little ball.

"You're sensitive. That's good. But now I'm not going to detain you any longer."

As he goes in to see Jim, I hear the music inside stop.

Jim and Sabina remain sitting in the chapel after the others have gone back to the wards. Edvard is standing at the door with his back to them, waiting. Sabina points at the angels on the ceiling.

"After Michelangelo had finished one of his angels, he looked at it and asked, 'But why aren't you alive?'"

Jim glances over at Edvard.

"Come on. He's waiting for us."

"Edvard's no angel, he's an arsehole. There isn't a doctor who doesn't ask after five minutes if we can go out together. I'm the best they've got."

"I think he's interesting."

"It's obvious what you think. The first time I saw you I knew that you and Edvard shared the same innocence. You don't know anything, either of you."

She presses up against him and carries on talking into his sweater.

"You like being here, don't you?"

"Yes, I do. It's strange. Or is it strange?"

"Well, yes, it is a bit strange, but I've known stranger things. Disappointed?"

Jim smiles and pushes her away.

"Shall we go?"

Edvard is standing absolutely still by the door; the only movement is the smoke rising slowly from his cigarette. He is illuminated by the last of the sunlight.

"I can see inside you," Sabina says, moving back into his arms.

"What can you see?"

"A heart that is too large. There isn't room for it. You drink to make it smaller. I'm sorry, but that won't help. You could pull out all your insides, and your heart as well, and you would still hurt. What are you doing tonight?"

Jim clasps his hand to his chest.

"I'll be lying, looking at the moon."

"Do you want to come out with me instead?"

"Where?"

"To a party."

"How could we go to a party, Sabina?"

She puts her hands over his eyes, kisses him and whispers:

"Do you want to go out, or don't you?"

"Too bloody right I want to go out."

"Okay then."

Edvard flicks away his cigarette and turns to look at them.

"Are you coming?"

At the red light by Bromma Church Edvard turns to look at Jim in the back seat.

"Fru Hjertén painted the angels when she was here. Do you like them?"

"It would be hard not to like them."

Sabina's eyes catch his in the little mirror she is holding in her hand, like a flash of lightning within him.

"But there's always a hassle with angels in hospital," she says.

"Why?"

Her glance slides away. The mirror disappears into her bag.

"It can't be prettier in hospital than it is outside," she says.

"I want to show you something," Sabina says, dragging me with her. "May I borrow her for a moment?" she asks, into the air.

I turn round to see who she is talking to, but there is no-one there. We go up some stairs and along a corridor that looks as though it is tipping up. It is amazing that the medicine trolleys are still standing by the walls and not rolling away, because everything seems to be sloping. Inger Vogel comes along with her enormous bunch of keys and opens up for us. I catch a glimpse of Jim in the dayroom before we go into Sabina's room, where a woman is sitting on the next bed squeezing a spot at the top of her plump arm. She has greasy hair plastered around her puffy face and looks briefly at me before continuing to pinch her arm. Sabina hands me a little package she has hidden in the mattress. I can see that it contains a piece of jewellery, a fine gold chain.

"Can you drop this off in Albano for a friend of mine?"
"Okay."

Then she loses herself in her powder compact. I stay for a while, but when I realise she is not there anymore, I go off to see Jim.

Outside, the clock in Hedvig Eleonora Church strikes four. The first birds can be heard far away, on their way back after the night. At dawn there are so many, circling round the tower like an ominous cloud; I often sit by the window and watch them while I wait for Marion to wake.

Jim rises to his feet and stands by the door to the balcony.

"Remember this, Jackie, if you ever end up in a mental hospital, you must always make sure you shack up with the ward nurse."

"Okay . . . Why?"

"Because she's the one who controls the medicine cupboard."

"I'll remember that," I say, laughing. "But there aren't any mental hospitals anymore."

"No, that's true. And I suppose Inger Vogel is long gone."

---

The night before he returns to Cariño, I lie awake. At first light I dress and go out for a while. Jim is sleeping on a thin mattress by the cot, and when I peep into the room I can see that Marion has got down beside him. He is lying with one leg over Jim's chest and his face pressed against his shoulder, just as he does when he sleeps with me.

Jungfrugatan is deserted, the asphalt is wet, and a grey light hangs like fine rain under the lamp posts. The wig-maker is already at his table, working in the faint glow from a bulb. I stop and watch him for a moment before I walk on. He is sitting in a small circle of light, slowly plying a needle up and down in an ash-blonde wig. Inside the church of Hedvig Eleonora the lights are on, as always, and right at the front an old woman is sitting alone, asleep under the angels, plastic bags at her feet. She does not wake up when I go past. Next to the baptistry is a glass coffin which was not there before. Inside the glass lies a child, asleep; it must be a doll, but she looks so real. Her body is covered with white feathers that constantly move in an unseen wind, even though the air in the nave is absolutely still. I stand and gaze at her for a long time. The gentle stirring of feathers makes it look as though she is breathing.

When I come out into the daylight again the men are already in their places on the benches in the square. From a distance they look like a bevy of large birds huddling to keep warm in the cold winter. A thin one, bearded and wearing a sailor's jacket, sits apart from the others, a small suitcase at his side. He has been sitting there drinking in the square for so long that we have started to speak to one another. Every time I walk past he waves to me to come and sit beside him. Sometimes I do, I sit for a while with my shopping bags, listening to him, and I smell the stench of death stream from the blackness of his mouth.

"What have you done with Biscuit?" he asks.

"Biscuit's still asleep," I say, pointing towards Jungfrugatan.

"Tell him to come down and I'll show him how to fold a proper sport plane."

His eyes are watery blue and quite clear, and he has in common with so many alcoholics a humility in the face of death, a particular gentleness. If they stop drinking, it evaporates; they grow hard and cold, leaving just the recklessness given them by drink – their only protector.

In the apartment Jim and Marion are already awake, sitting at the kitchen table in the glare of the silvery-cold light. They look as though they are contained within their own summer, their heads bowed over one of Marion's crashed helicopters. I stand in the doorway watching them for some time before they notice me.

"Look, Mum, my Goldwing can fly again!" Marion shouts, and he lifts up his arm to dispatch the little aircraft across the room.

＊＊＊

I have been on my own with Marion. I left Rickard when I was pregnant; I knew that I would never be able to share a child with anyone. Rickard used to come and see us, but he has not for a long time now; I think it made him depressed to be a stranger here, to be on the outside. In the delivery room I asked the midwife to leave so that I could be alone with the pain, and I would not allow anyone to visit afterwards. Every night I lay awake looking at Marion lying there in the dark, his legs drawn up under his stomach like a little frog.

When we came down in the hospital lift, Lone was outside, waiting for us under a yellow umbrella, clutching a gigantic bunch of winter roses to her chest. She went home with us in the taxi; I was in the back seat with Marion wrapped in a shawl. On the way home she said she had dreamt about me the night Marion was born, a dream in which I was little again and had a temperature and a racing pulse, and she had left me on my own with Jim, and I had shouted to her in the dream, and she could not answer. It was raining when we reached my street, a hushed November rain, and I stood on the pavement, cradling Marion, as I watched Lone's yellow umbrella disappear into the crowd. I would not let her come up with us to the apartment.

*

The first night with Marion I dreamt that my milk turned black, that it flowed out of me like thick burnt sugar and yet I made him suckle. I could not breastfeed him after that, I was so scared it would make him ill. Rickard came to visit us after a few days; his eyes filled with tears when he saw Marion, he lifted him carefully from my arms and kissed his little head before giving him back to me.

"You're not coming back, are you, Jackie?"

He looked at me as if he could see right through me. And then he left. It was as though all the darkness between us had never existed, the men I met in secret and my abrupt departure, the nights I sat on the balcony with my great stomach, watching the sun rise above the trees, my decision to be on my own with Marion.

I could not bear Rickard's eyes on me; it was like being in a tight wet sweater that I could not wriggle out of. He still said I was beautiful. He still said it when it was all too late, when I had long since destroyed everything.

Jim is sitting at the piano, playing something for Marion. It is loud and fast, as if he thinks he is playing for the last time, and it is Mozart again, the same repertoire he trots out whenever he comes anywhere near a piano. I remember how amazed I was at the melodies Jim conjured out of the piano when I was a child, how I could stand in the thunderous wave that crashed over me and feel the notes sweep through my body, how they soared and dipped inside me like wings. When I touched the keys nothing like that ever happened. A single note and then another single note and then nothing.

The music flowing from the piano and through the open window onto Jungfrugatan, where the snow has begun to fall, makes the room feel bigger. Marion's little helicopter propels itself across the room like a dragonfly, and on his face is an expression I have never seen before: as he stands with the miniature transmitter in his hand, following it with his gaze, hypnotised by the rise and fall in the music and the gentle humming from the helicopter, it looks as though he is at once both child and man. When I see him there in the light, I understand for the first time that he is his own person, and that there will be many others who will bring him happiness and heartbreak. It will not just be me.

"Mum, what happens if everything disappears?" Marion sometimes asks as he drifts off. He presses his feet against me while he dreams, as if to reassure himself that I am there.

"If everything disappears, then you and I will still be here."

"But how can it be that we exist if everything else has gone?"

"I don't know. It just is."

When Rickard fell asleep in the evenings, I would go out. He always slept soundly and without suspicion; he reckoned that when he awoke everything would be the same as it was before. I walked around in the night, May became June and then July, and I had just discovered I was pregnant. The streets were full of night-walkers; I was not the only one alone that summer during which the days never seemed done and a roseate glow shimmered over the city until long after midnight. I had not said anything to him about the child. I thought all along that I would get rid of it. I had even been to the clinic; I kept making new appointments, but I could not bring myself to go in, I could not kill something that had come to me. At dawn I walked back home and crept in behind his back. By the time the alarm went, I was sick with exhaustion. I was so scared it would be a girl, that she would be like me. When Marion arrived it was as if the ground suddenly felt firmer beneath my feet, as if gravity governed me as well.

---

"Jim, do you think my tree is still standing in Observatorie-lunden Park?"

"I don't know. I don't recognise Stockholm anymore. But we can go and have a look, if you like. I still don't know what I'm going to do with the rest of my life, though. I suppose when you die, the problem is partly solved."

"Only partly?"

Jim laughs.

"Well, or altogether."

That evening we walk up to the Observatory. Jim is sober again and his voice is perfectly gentle, as it was before, long ago. All at once he sounds like the Jim I find so hard to remember, the way he was before the alcohol, before the devastation; if there really is such a thing as *before*.

# UNDER THE MIGHTY SKY
# (DESIGN FOR A HOSPITAL)

A small group of people has gathered in the quadrangle outside the Clock-House at Beckomberga to raise a toast to the new hospital. The summer of 1932 is unusually cool, a cold spring has become autumn by the end of August. There are no inmates here yet; the first patients will not arrive for a few weeks. In the little company, raising their champagne glasses, are other representatives of the Medical Council, a number of doctors, officials and politicians, as well as the architect Carl E. Westman. Above: occasional clouds over a low, bile-coloured sky and only sparse foliage so far. Newly planted Japanese trees and exotic shrubs stick up out of the ground here and there, delicate and insecure, looking disorientated after their long journey across the world. In the failing afternoon light, this assembly of goodwill is waiting to celebrate the hospital's inauguration. Distant thunder can be heard, violet clouds roll in over Clock-House Park, and instead of raising their glasses to one another they raise them to the amber sky. A curious gesture, as if someone up there were taking part in the ceremony, or at least overseeing the work going on below. Brief applause, and then someone comes out with a silver platter of chicken sandwiches. Westman is slightly preoccupied; in his thoughts he is already on his way elsewhere. In his head he is sketching new buildings, impatient for the ceremony to be over so that he can drive back to the office and be reunited with his drawing board. His large curly head is filled with ideas of a new world in which illness no longer exists, no more confusion or poverty or any of the humiliation that has always surrounded the sick and the lost. Someone from the committee makes a short speech about the new hospital, about cleanliness, order and beauty; here the sick will want for nothing.

It is the birth of the welfare state out of darkness. A castle at the bottom of the world that is really a prison, a palace for the crippled and the hopeless where they can stumble around in dingy, motionless light, alone, locked up, forgotten. A clean, brightly lit hospital ward pushing out of the ground like a foetus from blood and membranes; a palatially majestic hospital building where only forest has been before: birds, trees, sky, water.

During that first year, 1932, 600 people are admitted to Beckomberga. Three years later there are 1,600 patients and with over 800 resident staff it resembles a small town.

# DARK SPRING

"Do you remember the tree you planted for me in Observatorielunden Park, and it flowered the winter that Jim went to Beckomberga?"

Lone looks at me in another dream. In my dreams I call out to her, she never calls to me.

"I don't think it's still there. They cut it down when they redid the park at the Observatory."

"But do you remember, it flowered in the middle of winter, and suddenly it had tiny pink and yellow blossom all over?"

"It didn't flower," Lone says, pushing a strand of hair away from her face. "It was your dad who'd hung up paper lanterns when he was drunk a few weeks before he went into hospital."

I have always thought they were winter blooms, always thought it was a miracle that they suddenly came out in the frost. I thought they were Chernobyl flowers.

"Why did he do that?"

I zip up my quilted jacket and blow on my fingers, which feel numb with the cold.

"He probably wanted us to see that he was sad. And maybe you're mixing up Observatorielunden Park with the flowers in the hospital park."

"Maybe. And when the trees blossomed there, I started going by myself."

The liquid in the little syringe is golden in the bright sunshine. A doctor who is not Edvard is pressing Jim's head into the grass, while Inger Vogel gives him an injection which quietens his body. I have forced the sleeve of my jumper into his mouth, waiting for Edvard's arrival, but he does not come.

"Go," Inger Vogel says, looking up at me, "you've got to go home now, Jackie."

"But I can stay," I say, wriggling out of my jumper without dislodging it from his mouth. Jim looks as though he is asleep on the grass now, his breathing steady, like waves gently breaking on a beach. A streak of blood over one cheek. We sat looking at a book when he fell. A book about trees that he had borrowed from Edvard; we were on the page for the king-wood tree, the one that bursts into leaf last and loses them first. The tree of doom with its enormous roots that grip the earth like dragon's claws.

He opens his eyes and lies on his back, looking up at the treetops, his gaze unmoving, just a certain faint light that transcends his darkest stare. I touch his hand tentatively. It is cool but not cold. A soughing in the leaves above. Inger Vogel wipes away some of the blood with the hem of her skirt.

"Every angel is a terrible angel," he says, and turns his head away from me.

And then to Inger Vogel:

"Tell her to go. She can come back tomorrow."

When they carry him away I take my bag and leave.

———⟨∞⟩———

The next time I see Sabina she is sitting on the steps, smoking. She is paler than last time, her skin smooth and moist, and her hair seems to be lighter than before, duller, the same colour as old dishwater, as if something inside her is gradually making her fade until she disappears altogether.

"Your dad's okay now."

"Is he?"

"He hit his head, that's all. It happens to everyone. You have to knock off the tablets and stuff slowly. You can't just stop straight off. Something will give. I don't know what it is, but it's something. The big bad something."

He sits at the piano in the lounge and tears stream down his face as he plays. Inger Vogel sits beside him, making notes with a large red pen. The sunlight touches them alone; everything else is in shadow and they look as though they are lit up from within. I watch them for a moment before I walk away.

On my way out I meet Edvard.

"Don't you ever get too hot in that fur jacket?"

Everyone asks about the fur, as if it were more important and more fascinating than anything else in the world.

"Have you seen my jumper?" I ask instead.

"We threw it away. It was completely ruined."

He rests his hand between my shoulder blades, the same place as before.

"Are you okay, Jackie?"

"I'm okay."

The old man in the too-small jacket stops me as I leave. He looks ancient, as if frozen in another age. His hair has been slicked down and everything he has on looks well pressed: the little sports jacket and the enormous trousers held up by a pair of bright red braces.

"Has anyone phoned me?" he asks, staring with eyes that are yellow and watery. He looks frightened; his large hand shakes as he lifts it.

"Ask Inger Vogel," I say. "She knows everything round here. She's sitting in there by the piano."

Sabina appears from nowhere and takes his huge hand in hers.

"No-one's phoned you, Olof."

Jim leaves the chessboard and offers me a tattered packet of cigarettes.

"Do you smoke, Jackie?"

"Not yet," I say, although I have been smoking since the winter. I started when we were here the first time, when Lone had begun smoking again.

A shadow crosses his face, as if a bird were swiftly passing overhead.

"I'm sorry. Of course you don't."

"I thought I might start," I say, touching his arm. He looks at me and laughs, and I love it when he laughs, when the light finally enters his eyes.

"I think you should. It's never too late to start smoking."

"When I was little I used to think I would smoke the same brand as you. Prince Lights."

"And now?"

"Hobson. Everyone at school smokes them."

Above us immense clouds are gathering, charcoal-grey virgin clouds, stray mother clouds, every possible rare cloud formation that I have never seen anywhere else, and the stars here are out even in the afternoon. We stand in huddles by the chessboard outside the Clock-House, watching Jim and Sabina playing with enormous pieces that look as though they have been made for giants. While they play they are bathed in a circle of light. For long periods they remain still, staring at the chessmen, like two beasts of prey, each waiting for the other to attack first. Sabina peers into the twilight, taking an inordinately long time before she makes her next move. Sometimes she delays so long that Jim grows nervous and loses his concentration when it is at last his turn.

"Checkmate, you clown."

Sabina usually wins. She is quicker, colder, she is sheer mathematics. She laughs at Jim each time he loses and grabs hold of him from behind when he slings the chess pieces into the bushes. Jim plays as he lives, without considering, without strategy, without a thought for the future.

The light is soft and shimmers like gold and Edvard comes past and stops to play for a while. Playing for stakes is forbidden, everyone knows, but Edvard ignores the heap of coins and cigarettes lying right next to the chessboard. Jim and Sabina are the only ones who never play for money; for them it is about something else, about love, about loneliness, about freedom. And in the faint and remarkable starlight, the star of Bethlehem and Mizar, all that exists on this planet on evenings such as these in Clock-House Park, where guard dogs bark in the distance, is Jim and Sabina, aglow in the last of the early summer light, unless it comes from inside them. They are contained within themselves and by the numbness they provide each other. And this is how it is: suddenly a girl rushes away across the grounds and a flock of white-coated nurses run after her and wrestle her down onto the grass. We see it happen and scarcely pay heed, but it is always there, this threat of being transferred or locked up or sedated. I am the only one free to leave, and all I want is to stay.

"The king's value is infinite," Sabina says, and walks away.

Edvard is squatting in front of me on the grass. There is something solitary about him. I have noticed that he stays behind at the hospital late into the evening.

"Do you want a lift home?"

Music pours out of the car radio, and the smell of leather burnt by the sun and the whiff of petrol are soporific, like the warm purr of the engine. When we pull out of the gates Sabina is standing by the gatehouse with my hat on her head.

"You forgot this," she says, when I have wound down the window. As I reach for it, she takes my wrist and kisses it. She pushes something hard into my hand, a roll of banknotes. A little rose has been tucked between the notes.

I drop off and when I awake I meet Edvard's eye in the rear-view mirror.

"I dreamt I was falling," I say, into the air.

"You don't need to be afraid of falling. In a dream you can fall without hurting yourself. Without bruises and scratches afterwards."

His look in the mirror is dark, as if the pupil fills the whole eye, but his voice is gentle and warm, as usual.

"Do you know about lucid dreams, Jackie? They're dreams where you can control what happens, yourself. You can learn how to have dreams like that. They'll be beneficial for you."

"Do you think so?"

"Absolutely."

When I turn round in the doorway he is still sitting, watching me, holding a lit cigarette. The door slams behind me and as I go up the stairs I hear the engine start up outside.

I leave Sabina's package in the entrance to the Natural History Museum. A girl with silver hair is sitting there selling tickets. She takes the package from me without a glance, as if I were invisible. Her hair shines in the darkness inside her little box; I have never seen anyone like her before. I cannot stop gazing at her, a pale vision behind the glass, like some exotic animal. After a while she pushes over another package. It smells sweet and slightly sour, like incense. I stuff it into my pocket at once, not looking at it, and retrace my steps over the cold stone floor. I am a courier now, one of Sabina's swift arrows.

# THE LAST PATIENT
# (STILL IN THE LIGHT)

"What do you think about your time here, Olof?"

Dr Janowski pushes a box of pastilles across the table. Olof takes a sweet and leaves it on the table in front of him.

"Here in the hospital?"

"Yes."

"I don't know. There was never any other time. I've been here all my life."

"So it's been home for you?"

"No, not home. But I had my bed here, and all my things, and I had my friends. And you . . . After my childhood, I never had a home."

"Do you think that anything could have been different here?"

Olof puts the sweet carefully into his mouth and sucks it.

"I would have liked to go to Dad's funeral. Seeing as he never visited me here, I would have liked to go."

"I understand. Sometimes we never get round to saying goodbye."

"No. And now they've all gone. Mum as well."

"Yes."

A breeze whispers through the building, as if all doors have been opened wide to the night.

"Mum came and sat knitting for a few hours at the start. She was knitting for me and Sixten. Sixten and I used to stand underneath the hydropower station at the falls, listening to the huge roar, and watching the smoke rise up from the matchstick factory above. Mum's dad and Uncle Karl and Dad's dad came home smelling of sulphur and phosphorus. At seven o'clock they marched in through the gates and at six in the evening they were let out into the light again, their faces black and soot in their hair. When we saw them coming we ran down to meet them. When I grew up I did the same thing. We walked into the dark early in the morning and were spat out into the light when the sun was going down."

Dr Janowski leans back in his chair and clasps his hands behind his head.

"I thought we ought to talk a little bit about what happens next."

"Next?"

"Tell me about your plans."

Olof's face brightens.

"I'm going to go to Sabbatsberg Hospital every day and I'm going to live with my brother and his wife at the beginning. Right? Is there something else I've forgotten?"

"That sounds a good plan."

"They're old as well. I don't think they'll manage much longer. And I've got my medicine."

"Yes, you've got your medicine."

Olof leans forward and lowers his voice.

"And I'm counting on Olof Palme. He's my last hope."

"What do you mean, you're counting on Olof Palme?"

"I don't know, I just am. I believe Olof Palme thinks about us, all the people who aren't very well off."

# THE TELEPHONE CONVERSATION (STOCKHOLM–CARIÑO)

When I hear Jim's voice on the telephone coming down the wires that run along the motorways of Europe, I sense how it mellows when he realises who is ringing.

"Oh, is that you? How are you?"

"I'm fine. Marion has started school. How about you?"

"Same as ever . . . What's the point of it all?"

He speaks for a while about the house over there, about the orange trees and about a woman called Magda who helps him with the cooking and cleaning; we talk about how quickly Spain is changing nowadays, how every day more and more people are forced to leave their homes.

"Europe will go under in the end," he says, gloomily. "Grand Europe will be turned into the world's backyard." Maybe he thinks of himself as Europe.

When he has finished I come clean, tell him I would like to read his medical records from Beckomberga. In my hand are Sabina's pearls, and as we talk I drop them one by one onto the desk, and then I pick them up and let them fall again.

"Of course you can read my records. I have no secrets from you," he says immediately, without thinking.

"Would you like to read them too?" I ask.

"I'd rather not."

"But I may?"

"Yes, it's your life as well. You were there, and you've always known more about me than I've known myself."

The sun is going down behind the church. A cold white winter sun. I have been putting off this call, lifting the receiver many times and then replacing it.

"But I don't even know where the records are. I don't know how I can help you."

I tell him that all the documentation relating to Beckomberga is preserved in an archive just outside Stockholm, that throughout the cold spring I have been there reading the medical records and registers from the hospital's first decade. After being closed for seventy years, the records up to 1943 have been made public.

"What's in the records?"

"All sorts of things. Photos of all the patients. The youngest is only six, a boy with final-stage syphilis."

"Poor kid."

"There were no medicines, nothing. Most people died in there."

"It wasn't like that in my time. It was a different kind of hospital. I loved being there. But I remember the screams at night, I remember the old women and men who'd been in for years, remember them wandering around in the exercise yard by themselves."

There is still a little light from the sun through the trees. They look so small from here, tiny matchstick trees. By my feet lies

Marion's radio-controlled Zeppelin; the batteries are strewn across the floor and it looks as though he has opened up the back and tried to repair it.

"When I tell people you were at Beckomberga, they always think you're dead," I say.

"Why do they think that?"

"That's probably what Beckomberga meant to people, like all the old mental hospitals, a place apart from the rest of the world, a place no-one ever came out of alive," I say, catching an escaping pearl before it falls to the floor. The pearl is dark blue in my hand, cold, bright cobalt.

"In summer, when you come to Stockholm, maybe we could drive out to the archive and collect your records together?"

A long silence at the other end. The muffled sound of cicadas. My eye follows an aeroplane moving slowly in the distance. A faint line across the sky, disappearing behind bare trees. Jim's voice sounds close, but he is already infinitely far away.

"But I don't know if I'm coming back to Stockholm," he says finally. "You haven't forgotten?"

Bells ring in Hedvig Eleonora Church and a white trail behind the aircraft runs like a seam through the blue until it thins and evaporates. There is something about the perspective – from my window it looks as though all these machines are plunging towards the earth. When I say nothing Jim continues and from over there he sounds ethereal, a white feather floating in his voice.

"Bring Inspector Belmondo with you and I'll show him the ocean. If you come, I'll write a letter of authorisation for you to take to that archive."

# WINTERSON'S TOYS

The clasps in Lone's hair are shining like glow-worms at night. A solitary wisp has strayed from her bun and is hanging in a curl in front of her face. The gold beetle clip, the pearl clip, the same as always. She looks down at her watch, a slender silver one she has had for as long as I can remember, and then up at the old hospital clock. In my dream we are standing outside Stora Mans in the raw cold.

"That must have stopped. Mine says nearly eight. What time is the bus?"

"Every half hour," I say. "We can leave whenever we like."

"It'll soon be dark."

"Can't we stay for a while?"

"If you want."

Her gaze follows something I cannot see, a fleeting shadow that disappears between the trees, a tiny bird or a moth. She reaches for her camera instinctively, as always, before stopping herself.

"You didn't like visiting him, did you?" I say.

"No, I didn't."

"You went away. To the Black Sea."

"Yes."

"And I started coming on my own."

"Yes. I hated the smell of illness here, the gritty white smell of institution. I felt sick as soon as I came into the hospital grounds."

"I did too, but I got used to it."

"You've never been afraid of anything, Jackie."

"I have. I was as scared as you, but I did it anyway."

Her hand rests on the camera.

"Why did you do it?"

"I didn't want him to be alone."

When she looks at me, her eyes are dark.

"I was alone too, Jackie."

On only one occasion does Jim ask to leave the hospital. He has been transferred to the medical ward, but once a day he climbs the many stairs up to the attic, where Edvard is, to talk about his life.

Edvard stands by the window, looking out at the snow and exposed patches of earth in Clock-House Park. He has just told Jim about his first post-mortem, a girl he knew from grammar school who had committed suicide and whom he found placed in front of him in the dissection class.

"It was the first time I touched a girl without clothes. The light, curly pubic hair, the pink spots on her breasts and the rigid, dead face seemed to belong to two entirely different women. When I examined her body before the post-mortem, I could feel the organs under her skin, she was so thin. The liver, gall bladder, spleen, kidneys."

His eyes fill with tears at the memory of the girl's stricken, naked corpse. Jim has nothing to add about girls with two faces.

"I don't want to stay here with all these nutters. I don't think it's going to make me better."

Edvard turns to look at him in astonishment, as if he had forgotten Jim was in the room. A part of him is still in the classroom, surrounded by metal bowls with organs and the sweet smell of intestines.

"We're all crazy, Jim," he says. "I'm crazy. You're crazy."

"And how do you know I'm crazy?"

Edvard's smile lights up in front of Jim, like an electric bulb in a darkened room.

"You have to be. Otherwise you wouldn't be here."

Each time I walk in through the hospital gates the rest of the world slides away, like the tide that recedes to lay bare another shoreline, like uprooted trees in Judarn Forest where the larvae crawl. I hurry across the quadrangle to the birch trees outside Jim's ward, and I imagine myself lying here on the grass one day, as Sabina does, with a huge book open in front of me. She is a picture of the future: her clarity and beauty.

"Hello, Sabina."

She does not answer and looks at me as if I were a tree or flower. Gently I put a little bag next to her hand.

Heat rises from the damp earth and the first pale butterflies flit between tall blades of grass. It is as if there were only one season here: the warm, unrelenting rain of this summer, and the shadows from the motionless treetops above, no wind, no time, no future. Jimmie Darling often goes around in a group with other patients when I am there; he belongs to the hospital now. And maybe he has never belonged to us; he has never belonged to me, anyway, even if he might have been Lone's once, a long time ago.

I am perspiring in my fur coat but I do not want to take it off, and the flowers in the trees are as big as my head, white petals swaying in the humid air. Some of the trees are very old, a thousand years or more, and some quite young.

"So many young trees have perished this year," Jim says, and then he starts to weep again. "It's the end of the future."

In the distance I can see him in the sunshine outside Stora Mans; he is holding court again on the slope under the birch trees, in the cold white light. When I come closer I can see that Edvard and Inger Vogel and a few others are listening to him. I have been let in through the electric gates by a sleepy watchman, I have crossed the large quadrangle and passed the fountain at the main entrance and this is the moment before he sees me; when he does catch sight of me he will throw back his head and laugh, as he always does.

"Jackie, you little idiot! Are you here again?"

I wait for a second in the shifting shadows of the birch trees before making myself known to him and the little white-coated audience, because I want to observe him without him seeing me, I want to keep the moment to myself for a while, I want to be outside the light.

There is only the shadow and the faint rustle of birch leaves, and Edvard and the others bursting into laughter all of a sudden. Every time this happens, Jim's face softens and the strained expression smoothens out, for a few seconds the anxiety vanishes. As long as people are laughing, there will be no more questions, for an instant he is blameless. And quickly, as if they had never been there, the little group around him scatters and disappears over the quadrangle and is swallowed up by one of the huge buildings. I step out of the shadow and when Jim sees me he opens his arms to me.

"You little nutcase, are you back again?" he calls. "You need to be careful, Jackie. Soon you'll be as nutty as me."

Sabina is sitting on the grass a little way off, searching for something in the enormous bag she always carries with her. Her fair hair hangs down her back.

"Do you know what time it is?" I ask, for something to say.

"No idea. Half past three."

"It's always half past three here."

"That's because everything bad always happens at half past three."

"Does it?"

"Yep. At half past three He was impaled on the cross by the Spear of Destiny. At half past three I fell. No-one caught me."

"Ah, right. I was just thinking I should try and catch the bus."

"One's just gone."

"It doesn't matter. I'm only going home."

I always miss the bus here. As soon as I arrive, I forget the time. I become submerged in something and forget everything outside.

"Be glad you've got stuff on the outside," she says, as if she can actually read my thoughts. She continues, "I was up looking at the clock with Edvard once, when it was still working. The hands were as big as me. That clock looked as though it belonged to giants when you saw it close up."

"Are all the doctors here like Edvard?" I ask.

"Edvard's okay, but he doesn't know anything about life. He's only in charge of Ward 6, and Ward 6 is something Chekhov invented."

In the evenings they get away from the hospital. As the electric gates open and let the car through, the first bottle is uncorked in the back, always champagne that has been chilling in the cellar during the day. Edvard drives across the bridges in the direction of the city, through sleeping residential areas and streets. Sometimes a girl from the ward is already waiting in the back; sometimes it is Sabina, sometimes someone else, often half comatose with medication. Birch trunks shimmer in the twilight; India-ink skies dappled with pink and yellow, stray wisps of cloud, birds, a haphazard drawing of the heavens. Edvard is convinced it is good for the patients to get out of the ward every so often.

"One night beyond the confines of the hospital makes you human again," he says.

Jim is given a crystal glass and in the glove compartment is a new shirt and a little bag of something that will make the night go faster. He sees the city pass by outside, men on their way home to their families, solitary women walking slowly along the streets, and sometimes, when they stop at a pedestrian crossing, waiting for the lights to change, he finds he is looking into the face of an old friend or colleague standing there, waiting. Once, by a crossing outside the Ministry for Foreign Affairs, he looks straight into Lone's face, before the car accelerates and drives away through light streaming out of clubs that have just opened their doors to the night.

Once in a while a girl has a breakdown during the night in the apartment on Lill-Jans Plan, and then she has to go back with them to the hospital at daybreak. "Winterson's toys" is what they are called, the girls who drift aimlessly around these parties, sometimes taking payment for their company, and when they fall over they go back with Edvard in the car, waking up later in an all-white room with his face hovering above them.

"Don't be afraid, sweetheart. We'll take care of you."

"Where am I?"

"Never mind about that. You don't need to think anymore, my dear."

*Jim: The girls stayed at the hospital for months. They were girls no-one missed. Much later I learned we were all called Winterson's toys, not just the girls. I changed my clothes on the way into the city. Edvard wanted us to talk about girls. He was always in love with one of the patients. None of the women at the parties interested him if they'd come from outside; for him there were only the patients. We drank copious amounts at these events; there was cocaine, grass, sleeping pills. He introduced me to beautiful rich people and somewhere out there in the city was what had once been my life. It didn't exist any longer. The only thing that did were these nights we drove out of the hospital grounds. The night Olof Palme died, lights were on in apartments long into the early hours. People stood at windows, raising their glasses.*

Some nights Sabina leaves the apartment on Lill-Jans Plan, her steps retreating down the stairs, and from the street she waves at Jim, who is sitting with some elderly women, regaling them with his stories about the hospital. It is like a game; if he can make them laugh he does not need to be afraid of them, of their wealth, of the ease with which they move. He always manages it; they chortle with their hands pressed to their lips until red patches appear on their necks.

"There's a whole world in the underground passages," he says. "Tree roots force their way down through the ceiling in some places. It's incredible. Orphan kids used to run around down there before. Now it's mainly Edvard riding around on his scooter."

"And Edvard lets you come out like this?"

He touches a woman's hand; the skin is wrinkled under the gold charms.

"Yes, as luck would have it."

On the way back a new girl is sitting in the back seat, looking out over the city, her eyes heavy. When Jim asks about Sabina, Edvard is taciturn.

"She'll come back. Sabina's never out for long. No more than a few days, at most."

"I thought she couldn't wait to get out."

Edvard gives a short laugh.

"That's what she thinks."

The Traneberg Bridge disappears in the quivering white light of dawn. It looks as though it leads nowhere, as though it has nothing to tether it at the other side. Jim closes his eyes and drops off. He is woken by guard dogs barking at the car. Edvard is sitting quite still beside him, looking out over Clock-House Park.

The car door opens in front of Sabina as she is on her way into Kungsträdgården Park; a voice she recognises, pale hands with a light smattering of freckles in the darkness of the coupé's interior, a wreath of smoke rising slowly to the roof. She is wearing a bright blue jacket over her jeans, it is early in the morning and she has been up all night counting stars. The sun filters through the trees as if through a magnifying glass; her hair is matted and dirty. In her veins the residue of a sedative that mixes with her blood and something else, something harder, crystalline, deadly, weightier than all love. The sky above shimmers gold; solitary birds fly between the trees.

"Will you come back with me to the hospital?"

"What am I going to do there?"

"Maybe you're tired. You might need some sleep."

"Can you help me with that?"

"You know I can."

"Death doesn't want me, anyhow."

---

"Come in for a moment, child," yells the shopkeeper, his enormous body blocking the doorway. I sidle into the darkness; the smell of death hits me and I draw it down into my lungs. The door closes behind us and each time I reach out my hand and touch something, he yells that I can have it. I ignore him.

"You look good in a hat. There are lots of hats that would

suit you. I have a very nice slouch hat from Tokyo you can have a look at."

He pats the fur coat gingerly, as if I were a real animal. When I say I am looking for something special, for a friend who is in hospital, he dashes through the shop. On his way he knocks things over onto the floor – fans and candlesticks and a naked dummy. I carefully pick up the fans and put them back. The mannequin is lying overturned in front of me, her arms and legs twisted in a strange position. I step over her to make my way further into the shop. The man is gone for a while, and then he appears behind the curtain with a globe in his hands. A cord trails behind him.

"This is what you need. He can have the globe."

He spins it with his fat fingers and they leave greasy marks on the oceans.

"It's yours if you want it."

I take it without looking at him and walk quickly towards the door. When I turn round he looks helpless, his hands outstretched.

"Wait a minute. I can give it a wipe."

"No need," I say.

"Is it your dad who's sick?" he asks suddenly, as if he knew me. Perhaps he sees everything that happens in the neighbourhood, perhaps he knows everything about the inhabitants of Kammakargatan.

"It's the Chernobyl cloud that's made him ill," I say, hurrying out of the shop.

"Oh, Jesus! How dreadful!"

131

His huge body begins to gather speed. He looks as though he wants to charge into my arms to comfort me. I slip out and let the door close behind me before he makes it.

In Adolf Fredrik's churchyard the gravestones shine like lone faces in the half-light. The evenings are so warm now, tropical.

I take the underground to Brommaplan and from there the bus to Beckomberga. At the hospital gates I am usually the only one to alight. Sometimes I have something for Sabina, a silver package or a little bag. I am becoming more and more attached to the hospital. I start to dream about it at night; I dream I am falling and I dream about Jim, that he is tumbling out of towering trees, that I have lost him before I have come to know him. I go to the hospital even when it is not visiting time and they let me stay. Edvard arranges it so that I can come and go as I wish; I eat with Jim and the others and I sit beside him and the rest of them in the day room when they play a game of dice in the evening. Jim is given permission to leave the hospital grounds and meet me at the bus stop, and he takes me back before dark. When the bus drives away with me into the violet dusk, he stands with his hand raised in farewell; I do not know if he is waving at me or shading his eyes against the light, but he is probably already somewhere else in his thoughts, for when I raise my own hand he remains motionless.

*

I stand in the hall in front of Lone. She must have been sitting in the dark, waiting for me, without switching on any of the lights. She takes off my hat carefully and runs her fingers through my hair, which is tangled and full of knots, and looks at me as if she can see right through me. Heart, lungs, innards, soul.

"You have a big heart," she says, putting the globe aside without looking at it.

"Have I?"

Instinctively I hold my hand in front of my chest so she cannot see it, my heart in its pericardium, hiding behind my ribs. A big heart sounds like a deformity, a defect.

"Tell me about Jim."

"There's nothing to tell."

"Tell me about the hospital."

I tell her that the flowers have come out in Clock-House Park now, that there are flowers everywhere in the soft grass, that the sunsets happen slowly and are almost never-ending, as if the last light could well be the first. When I say I have met Sabina, a shadow instantly passes over her face.

I like it when she tugs at my hair. It makes me drowsy and relaxed. My hair has become darker in the sun, the black sun of Lake Judarn. I wish she knew what the hospital looks like now, without the snow, without the darkness and the cold wind.

"You can go as often as you like, Jackie, but I want you to wake me when you come home. I want to know that you're lying in your own bed at night."

It is a mystery what she does with her hands; when I open my eyes my hair is perfectly soft and shiny again.

"Do you think summer will come again after Chernobyl?" I ask, so that she does not take her hands away.

"I don't know. I actually don't know if it will."

"When will we know?"

"Maybe never. Some things we never get to know. I'd like to go there to take some photographs."

"Isn't it dangerous to be there?"

"It's dangerous everywhere, Jackie."

# LIME TREE AVENUE
(MARION)

A pearly shimmer on the underside of the leaves on the trees. Marion and I walk in Clock-House Park all day. He runs around in his red woolly hat, zigzagging between the bare tree trunks. A short distance away the chessmen lie upturned and I miss Sabina, I miss all that is no longer here; I want her to be standing next to me with a smile, a white knight held to her chest. "Checkmate, Jimmie Darling."

At twilight Marion looks up at one of the windows in Stora Mans where a lamp always burns at night. Someone must be living in there, or at least returning each evening to sleep. The gold inscription gleams in the last of the light and the silvery rain; the Russian vine, trailing across the façade like a huge insect over the main entrance, was taken down a few weeks ago. Perhaps something is finally going to happen to the building now. The old hospital wings will be turned into residential dwellings, but they still stand unmoved and majestic in their beautiful muted crimson. Inside the glass doors it looks as though everything has been left as it was a decade and a half ago, as if the staff have just closed the door behind them and left. Signage is still visible in some places, only the bars at the windows and the fencing round the hospital grounds are gone, and parts of the fence are rolled up outside the former gate-houses on the old grass from last year.

\*

We stand in silence by the little pond, looking at the frozen water, and the cold surrounding us is like a clean, hard belt against our bodies: the smoke, the frost, the crystal clarity of the night. Marion runs away along the avenue that carries on forever between the ancient trees. I stay where I am and wait for him to come back. When I shut my eyes I can see Jim and Edvard leaving the hospital in the silver Mercedes. Smoke curls out of their cigarettes while they sit waiting for the guard to open the gates; and the sound of the birds, watching over everything from the trees. Sometimes she is there too, Sabina, half asleep in the back, a glass in her hand, her long white hair spread out like feathers over the back of the seat. And when Jim has buttoned up his shirt and inspected his face in the rear-view mirror, he takes his first swig of champagne; and then the faint swish of the electric gates can be heard as they finally open and let them out of the hospital park. They glide noiselessly away, along the lime tree avenue and further on up to the narrow lanes that lead from the hospital and then over the bridges towards the city lights.

"Shall we go home now, Mummy?"

He is cold and his hands are ruddy from making a little snow lantern right next to the pond, but we have no candle and no matches. I hold his hands between mine and try to warm them with my breath.

"I thought we'd go in for a while."

"What will we do inside?"

"I don't know. Walk around for a bit."

"Isn't it dark in there?"

"Yes, but it isn't dangerous."

"Are you sure?"

"I'm quite sure, Marion."

On the back of Stora Mans someone has carved a big heart on the red wall. A man alone, talking aloud to himself, moves across the quadrangle, and a woman walking her dogs, otherwise there is only us. The clouds are strangely low above us as we walk along in the chilly wind, pulling at locked doors. Some children come running out of the row of yellow buildings by the slope where we used to sit in the shade of the birch trees. They call to us and ask if we know that it was a mental hospital before.

"Yes," I call back. "My dad was here when I was little."

At my response, the children retreat and make off towards the avenue. We return to the chapel and the main building as the snow begins to fall, a fine April snow, and it feels as though it is snowing inside me when Marion unexpectedly manages to open one of the doors at the back. The pure smell of snow and light hits us, a soft and shadowy light of the subterrestrial, and an overwhelming sense of sadness when I step inside that hospital again for the first time in more than twenty years.

"Who's sick?" Marion asks, looking at me as only he does. No-one else has ever looked at me in that way; he believes in me, for everything.

"No-one's sick. The hospital's been closed for ages. Come on."

*

He disappears along the corridor with a white bird's feather in his hand. I hear him singing in the distance. The rain-shiny green colour that reminds me of light in a swimming bath is still there, and the dormitories remain papered in different patterns, peculiar to each room. It is as if you can see time pass: the '40s, '50s, '60s, '70s, '80s. Medicine trolleys against the walls, piles of glass shards on the floor from the smashed window, and the suspicion that we are not alone. I feel as if I am going to see Jim coming towards me, and Edvard in his flapping white doctor's coat. And I imagine that the old men from Jim's ward who stood smoking under the birch trees will be there again when I look out of the window; when I close my eyes I feel Paul's large warm hands around my neck, his breath.

"Time to fly, little butterfly."

People say that former patients keep returning to Clock-House Park at Beckomberga, that they stand under the trees with their hands pressed on the sun-bleached walls, as if the institution's heart were still beating within – a weak human pulse against my hand when I touch the faint blood-red colour of the façade. It is the shadows and voices of all those who were here once, rising and falling inside like trapped birds; and when I shut my eyes I see myself and Jim lying curled up, asleep, at the top beneath the hospital clock, under his rough winter coat.

We are alone in the world, as we have always been, alone with his misery. In his sleep he has his arms around my shoulders so that I do not feel the cold.

II

# THE SECOND CONVERSATION
## (THE ATLANTIC)

We land in Cariño at dusk, the hour when shadows fade and vanish, when the light becomes gentle and weightless in place of the harsh white Spanish sunshine. Marion is sitting quite still in the car, looking at the blue mountains. He is sucking his thumb again, and the little blister that healed a long time ago quickly becomes wet and sore once more. Between the palm trees are the outlines of flitting bats, swift black specks in the dim light, like fallen leaves blowing around in the night. Grass and trees are scorched by the sun and there is a feeling of desertion, of inhabitants having abandoned these parts. When Jim moved here a few years ago, everything was different, there was an optimism about the place. Now you seldom see people between the houses; just the sharp barking of wild dogs in the distance, and villas without roofs that will never be completed now the money has run out, naked concrete corpses cast out onto barren land.

Jim looks tired as he sits gazing out over the arid plain. The screeching of birds above us, their yellow undersides soaring across the last faint orange of the sky before night. At the round-abouts the faces of destitute girls are lit up by car headlights; they sell the only thing they have, their East European bodies.

After Marion has fallen asleep downstairs, we sit on the terrace in the dark. The pounding of the waves below us drowns out the soft music coming from inside the house, Bach's "Magnificat", which Jim plays over and over again. Every now and then he goes inside and moves the gramophone needle to the part called "Et Misericordia (and Mercy)". I recognise the repetition in his actions, a swirl of dark thoughts and dreams that pulls him down.

"So what happens now?" I ask.

"Sweetheart," he says, "you know how it'll end for me. Sixty Imovane tablets and a whole bottle of whisky and then I'll walk into the sea. There's not much time left."

The stars seem to have slipped slightly in the sky, and in the darkness we hear the ocean's breathing, which never stops, the heavy waves beating against the shore before they draw back into the deep.

"When are you thinking of doing it?"

"I can't say. It'll be like something falling, inside me. I can't give you time and place. There's no schedule, no charts."

"And what then?"

"You can spread my ashes in the Atlantic or fly me home to Stockholm. The grave where Vita and Henrik are in Skogs-kyrkogården is a family grave."

The balcony door is open and Marion's high-pitched voice can be heard from down on the beach where he is playing under the palm trees. The grass below my window is strewn with crashed white paper aeroplanes. I have been awake all night, but Marion has slept soundly and woken up excited to be by the sea. The minute he opened his eyes he began folding paper aeroplanes and then forgot them and ran down to the beach to search for stones and starfish. I walk down to where he is standing – a little way out on his slender legs in the hazy glare of the water – and then I lie down on a towel and read. When I glance up it looks as though he is standing in a vast mirror.

The only one in our family not damaged is Marion. He is perfect: slim legs, like matchsticks in his trainers, and a high rib cage in his chest, where you can see his heart beating when he lies on the sand beside me soaking up the sunshine, the roar of the Atlantic next to us. The smoothness of his stomach, his arms, and his hands that open and close like jellyfish when he is sleeping under the parasol. Lone says Marion got his eyes from me; she says it is like staring into my eyes as a child. Sometimes I have wondered if it really is possible to inherit the look in your eyes, if darkness is passed down.

Jim touches my shoulder. He has come down to the beach and been sitting beside me without my hearing him; I must have nodded off. I am woken by the brief smell of sulphur when he lights a cigarette. He gazes out over the ocean, to the blurry, quivering horizon where sea and sky meet. The sun burns through the parasol.

"It'll be as if I was never here, Jackie. And you'll manage.

You always have. I've never been someone you could count on. You know that."

The ocean is completely still and motionless. He continues slowly.

"The instant before it all goes black there's no fear, just a faint light at the edge of consciousness. If time no longer exists, then neither does suffering. If space has come to an end, there's nothing to be afraid of. It's a sort of paradise, Jackie. It's paradise that beckons."

We are walking under the palm trees, along the stone wall, back up to the house. Marion is running ahead with his red ball. The heat is like a barrier around us, impenetrable.

Twilight is so brief in Cariño, everything goes dark without warning. The evening light here is remarkable, subdued and ominous and weightless just before it vanishes into the sea. We are driving to Bilbao, where we will catch a flight to Madrid and then another to Stockholm. There is a strong smell of pine and salt in the air; the heat from the day lingers over the mountains like a trembling shroud. The palm trees race by on both sides of the road; in the distance the glint of huge heaps of salt. I meet Jim's eye for a second in the small rear-view mirror before I carry on staring out at the road. In the mirror his face is furrowed and lonely, marked by invisible pain.

A pale full moon has appeared from behind the mountains though the sun is still burning low in the sky; they are shining next to each other, brother and sister. Marion is sitting beside me, looking out at the mountains in the distance with a little fleck of saliva on his chin. I should ask Jim to stay, but I can already hear his laugh. Jim's laugh, breaking over me like cold waves. "Remember, Jackie, I have no-one to live for, no-one to love. I never have."

Instead I ask:

"And what shall I do with you if you fail and end up in hospital somewhere?"

"Nothing," he says, smiling at me in the rear-view mirror. "I would never fail."

"But you've wanted to die before," I say. "This isn't the first time."

"Trust me, Jackie. I know what I'm doing."

"Okay. Do as you please. You always have."


A short distance away a solitary flamingo lifts off, bright shimmering pink in the scorched light, as if it were on fire, a flame shooting out of the water, turning into some kind of flying angel. I lean my head back; it is like suffocation, this situation after a few days with Jim. The birds fly over the road in front of us, small white forms that almost hit the windscreen, they fly so close. Somewhere out there in the ocean is Vita's lonely body; I imagine her as still in her bright spring coat, which floats like a little parachute over her head. What did she and Jim do? Did they play the same game of death that we are playing now? Vita went without saying goodbye; maybe Jim knows no other way to leave. He has spoken before about her last days.

*Jim: All that spring I knew she would die. She lay on the sofa, drinking. I'd already planned how I would rearrange the flat after she'd gone. I would take her bedroom. It didn't happen. My brother and I moved to a new flat on Kungsholmen. I don't know where it came from; one day we'd simply moved in, suddenly there we were, surrounded by packing boxes. Vita and Henrik were both gone. As if they'd never been. A whole world disappeared with them. And when I saw photographs of Vita, she looked different, even though I'd seen those pictures thousands of times. She didn't look as though she'd ever been my mum.*

# THE BLACK SEA

Jim and Edvard are at the window, looking out over the tree-tops. Every aircraft descending to land at the airport draws one more line across the sky.

"Why do you think you're so sad, Jim?"

"Why am I so sad? Why are you so cheerful, Edvard?"

Edvard laughs his easy, ringing laugh.

"Yes, why am I so cheerful?"

"The world out there is done for, and you're alone in your great apartment. You've only got us. And we're all lunatics."

"I don't know that I would call you lunatics."

"You know what I mean. Hopeless."

"Not you. You have a vein of gold in you, Jim. Only you've no idea how to make use of it. Can't you tell me how it all began?"

"When I came into hospital?"

"Yes, or when you came into the world. The first story about you. There's always one."

"All I know is that Vita and Henrik took me straight from the maternity ward to Kungsgatan to celebrate. There were people dashing around everywhere with white flags in their hands and confetti swirling in the air like huge raindrops. You've seen the pictures."

"It was a beautiful beginning."

"You think so?"

"Yes."

"I don't know," says Jim. "There always had to be grand gestures. It wasn't enough that she had just given birth to her first child, she had to go to Kungsgatan because everyone else was there."

"But it must have made her happy that the war was over, that she had you in peacetime."

"Vita was exactly like me. Nothing could ever satisfy her. She wasn't happy before Father died either, she was just as unhappy when he was alive. He always tried to make her go with him into the light, but she wouldn't."

"Perhaps she couldn't. Perhaps there was nothing she would have liked more."

"It's possible. Every morning she put on her beige pleated skirt and set off for the city to work. I saw her pull a comb through her hair before she turned the corner. She was one of the first women in our neighbourhood to go out to work and I admired her for it. I saw the effort, I saw the tedium and doubt; I had no problem understanding all of that."

"And what about you, Jim? There must have been moments in your life when you were happy."

"Yes. I've never been as happy as I've been here in hospital."

"Come on, now," Sabina says, pulling him along towards the fence on the north side, on one of the unsupervised walks to the shop that they are allowed every day. After six months in hospital, Jim is granted more and more time out. They have waited impatiently by the main door with bow and arrows, as Inger Vogel approached down the corridor with a large bunch of keys bouncing against her hip. When they have negotiated the fence they run blindly through the trees.

They stop to shoot for a while before the sound of guard dogs barking in the distance reaches them. Sabina's precision is truly fantastic; the arrow whizzes through the air in a perfect arc and hits the tree trunk she has aimed for, and with every shot they go deeper into the forest. It makes her laugh when Jim's arrows pitch into the moss after only a metre or two, while the sound of the dogs draws nearer and nearer.

"You'll never make it, Jim, but you're okay all the same."

The noise of barking is everywhere now, like a wall. She fastens her little pocket mirror onto a tree trunk and stares at her face, as if her destiny were actually somewhere else, hidden behind the reflection that appears before her. She looks like a doll; the medication makes her eyes glazed, her face puffy. Jim stands behind her, gazing into the mirror. In the land of the mirror they are other people; there is no hospital, no rules, no future, only their two faces side by side.

The barking intensifies. Sometimes it sounds quite close, and then the noise abates; there must be a whole pack. He looks at her face in the mirror. She should have been examining her own face, but she is watching him; then she looks away, at the trees behind the mirror, the soft flowing light that streams down between the treetops.

"I've never met anyone like you."

"You should be pleased about that," she says, gently grasping his neck and pulling him towards her. "Do you know what Einstein's happiest thought was?"

"No idea."

"That she who falls is outside all laws. Because in falling she feels no gravity."

"I don't want you to fall, Sabina. I think I could make you happy."

"Everyone thinks that. You can't. Come on."

Sheltered by the branches, they lie down on the ground. The barking is nearer now, a fast, heavy pounding between the trees, and a chill of fear runs like liquid down his spine. Jim kisses her bare, freckled shoulder and thinks she is the most luminous person he has ever seen as she lies stretched out on the grass. He wakes every morning in the ward thinking she is the most beautiful person in the world.

"You're basically far too intelligent, Sabina."

"For whom?"

"For me. You ought to study."

"I did one term at university before."

"Did you? What were you studying?"

"Maths. Zoology. A short course about Foucault's pendulum."

"Why did you stop?"

"I started going to lectures early. We lived right next-door to the university. Instead of going to school, I sat at the back of the lecture theatre, listening. Every now and then I slept."

Jim strokes her hair.

"Sometimes I wish I hadn't gone to university. I'd have liked to play the piano, or write. I think I'd have been a different person if I'd done that."

She kisses him hard and then pushes him away again.

"You'd probably have been insufferable."

Afterwards she leans against a tree and shuts her eyes against the gauzy light.

"Jimmie Darling," she says, "are you coming with me now?"

The barking of the dogs is like a cold pulse through his body; they start to run through the forest and as Jim runs the vision of Lone's face floating in front of him makes him realise that he thought all along they would go back to the ward after an hour or two. When the dogs come racing through the trees he lets go of her hand and walks slowly in the direction of the guards with his own hands held up over his head.

*Jim: I watched her at the side of the road among the hair clips, blades of grass and black feathers, leaning against a tree; I watched her look in the mirror, I watched her as she stared at herself, and in the blank surface of the little reflection there was absolutely nothing, just emptiness. Sabina was my last great love. And yet I couldn't picture myself with her outside the hospital. I couldn't picture myself with someone like her at all. Feral, innocent, lawless.*

The pale sun disappears behind the tops of the trees on the other side of Clock-House Park. The sky is like the inside of a snail. Grainy golden light, the trees bare and black in the rain. Only Lone's coat shining white.

"Sometimes it feels as though I grew up in this hospital," I say.

"Yes, you always wanted to come. The minute you woke up in the morning you took off to the underground with a little sandwich in your hand. I don't even know if you went to school for a time, but you could miss as much as you wanted, you always did well."

"But not that well?"

"Your marks might have dropped a bit, but you've always been brilliant."

"So wasn't it strange? That I spent so much time at an old mental hospital?"

Lone looks at me for a long time before she answers; I watch her drift off in her thoughts and come back. Soon this dream will fade away; I wish I could keep hold of her a little longer.

"I don't know if it was so strange. You wanted to be close to your dad."

"But he was never really like a dad."

"What was he then?"

"That's what I don't know. He was something else."

"Why did you come here then?"

The sun is faint now, only gossamer threads of gold lingering in the sky.

"I thought I ought to bring him home to you."

"But I didn't want him. Had you forgotten that?"

"I think so."

We are sitting in the room with the institutional lighting and I have hidden my hands in the sleeves of my jumper, because I want Edvard to see as little of me as possible. I wish I could hide my face as well, but a face is always naked. I have put the globe on the desk. He is sitting in silence, tapping his pencil on the desk. The freckles on his hands look as though they have merged at points.

"Do you know what tune this is?"

"No idea. Is it even a tune?"

"Yes. 'Just Call Me Lonesome.' Elvis Presley."

"Ah."

The smile has died now and he is looking at me intently. During the night there has been a fire at the hospital; the acrid stench of smoke is still hanging over the grounds.

"Your dad's in no danger. He just had a dizzy spell."

"Okay. Can I go now?"

"Wait a moment, Jackie. Why do you come here so often?"

He continues to speak without waiting for my answer. It is always like that if you just pause long enough; people always have the answer to their own questions.

"I'm going to sort him out for you."

"Okay."

"Jim has lost something and he doesn't know what it is."

"Did he lose it now? Just now?"

"No, it was a long time ago. It's a feeling that has become an empty void."

"So, what do you do about a void like that?"

"Nothing."

"Nothing?"

"It's not just about you and Jim. The new world is closing around us like a cage. We're tossed between desire, paralysis, emptiness. And the illness absorbs even the most outrageous, monstrous events. Hiroshima. The great wars."

"I don't know if I understand," I say.

"Never mind. Neither do I."

"Can't I go and see Jim now?"

Edvard hesitates for a second.

"Jim isn't here at the moment, you understand."

This I do not understand at all.

"Where is he then?"

"He can't have visitors right now. If you can wait a few minutes, I'll give you a lift into town."

Clock-House Park is cloaked in a light mist when I come out again with the globe in my arms; a faint white sun, the sun that shines after a long fever. The men are standing under their clouds of smoke, as they have always done and always will. Faces without shadows: naked, honest, their eyes ablaze. They all want to touch my long, uncombed hair, my head, my soft clothes; I do not know whether they are blessing me or if it is something else, but I do not stop them. They always say the same thing when they catch sight of me.

"You shouldn't be here. This is no place for someone like you. With your fine fur coat and everything."

"But there's nowhere else in the world I want to be," I reply.

They laugh at my obstinacy. Only Sabina leaves me alone.

"Would anyone like this?" I say, holding out the globe. "There's a lamp with it."

The old man in the sports jacket reaches out his big gnarled hands.

"Can I have it?"

"Take it. The person it was meant for didn't want it."

Next to the chapel is a huge black car with white curtains inside the windows. A man in uniform I have never seen before is leaning over a newspaper he has unfolded on the bonnet. Sabina is sitting on a bench in the shade of a tree with a powder compact in her hand, examining her face in the tiny mirror. Perhaps she is hoping to find another face there if she looks long enough. Inger Vogel is in the shadow of a tree some way off, gazing across the park. When she turns I drop the little package onto the grass in front of Sabina, and quick as a snake she puts out her hand and snatches it up.

"Someone said there was a fire here in the night, that someone set fire to himself in the workshop," I say, to keep Sabina from walking off.

And then, when she does not reply:

"Was he alright?"

"She. It was a she."

"Oh. Was she alright?"

She looks up at me with her pale eyes and her pupils contract in the bright sunlight.

"Do you know that you remind me of someone? Someone I used to like a long time ago."

"Everyone always thinks I look like someone else," I say, "and then thinks it's unreasonable that it's only me."

Sabina laughs, fleetingly, like quicksilver.

"Just that I was happy when I saw you."

"I was only wondering if she was alright. The woman in the fire."

"Obviously she wasn't. But listen, it's me you're like. From before. You have swimmer's shoulders. I used to swim. Whenever I had the chance. I thought I would swim the Atlantic."

She rises from the bench and briefly touches my shoulder.

"Before you were –"

"Yes?"

"Before you were – I mean before you – before you came here?"

"No, it was something else, a long time ago. A way of moving through the world, a way of asking loads of questions I didn't actually want answers to."

"What kinds of questions?"

"The usual. It was just that I got stuck in them. I couldn't move on. You're the sort who moves on. And now some Frenchman has done it. In seventy-two days. From Osterville to La Belle Île. It's a physical impossibility, he would've had to swim eighteen hours every day. Most likely he sat drinking red wine in the escort boat."

Edvard is suddenly standing next to her with a dark smile.

"Where's your beau gone, Sabina?"

Edvard's silver car has been parked in the sun the whole day. The seat burns my bare legs. I fall asleep before we have even left the hospital grounds. I am woken by his eyes in the rear-view mirror. I have dribbled a bit on the seat, a strand of saliva; I wipe it off with my hand.

"How long have I been asleep?"

"A little while. Were you dreaming about something?"

"No," I reply quickly, "I think I've stopped dreaming."

"If you really want to influence your dreams you have to try and watch out for a bird in the next one."

"What do I do if I see it?"

"Follow it, that's all."

A flight of jackdaws takes off as one when I slam the car door behind me. For a moment the sound is deafening.

"What a fate for a girl."

Lone leaves the newspaper open on the kitchen table as a warning. Some plastic bags were found a few summers ago next to the motorway, not far from the place where we lived before. In them were the remains of a dead girl. A severed breast, arms and legs, but no head, no abdomen. When I look closer at the photographs in the paper her slender face seems to have been drawn with an immeasurably fine pencil and the gaze in her brown eyes is indecipherable. It is as if a beast of prey has caught her scent and torn her out of the world, as if invisible claws have ripped her apart from the inside, an in-human, nameless hunger moving like a predator through the city. The paper says the dismembering suggests a butcher or an architect or a doctor.

Lone tries to persuade me to go with her on her trip to the Black Sea, but I have other plans for the summer.

"What will you do all by yourself in the city?"

"I'll go and see Jim sometimes. I might visit Grandma."

"And friends?"

"You know I haven't got any. I like being alone."

She falls to her knees on the floor in front of me.

"Come with me. Just this once."

"No."

The next morning, she has gone. I open all the windows and let the cold air flood the apartment. I smoke one of her cigarette ends in the ashtray while studying the dead girl's face in the newspaper. A thin red lipstick line around the butt, the smell of summer, menthol and raspberries.

Before leaving she goes to the hospital alone to speak to Jim. I see her disappear along the street, leaning forward a little, as if walking through a storm. When she returns she is pale; she goes into the bedroom, opens a large suitcase, and fills it with all the things she loves. Blouses, books, shoes, and a medium-sized oval mirror that she intends to lug with her halfway round the world. Only Lone takes mirrors with her on her travels. Perhaps she is afraid she will forget who she is. Every so often she stops in mid-movement and stands for a long time in front of the window. The night is dark out there; it too is like a mirror.

When Jim comes out of Stora Mans he lights a cigarette. The match flares for a second before he throws it into a puddle. A greyish, dead light, as if the rain that has been falling for days has dulled all the colours. Lone sits and waits under a tree. Jim sits down on the bench beside her. This is how I imagine it.

"Hello, Lone. Are you off on a trip?"

"In a few days."

"Where are you going?"

"Odessa. I might go further on to the scene of the accident."

"Okay. Just one thing. I don't want Jackie to come here anymore."

"Why? She really likes coming."

"But I have nothing to offer her. If I can't see you, I don't want to see her either."

"You can see me. You can come to Kammakargatan whenever you want."

"But there's no love anymore?"

She is quiet for a moment and fiddles with the buckle on her handbag. Then she looks up and meets his gaze.

"It's a long time since I loved you, Jim."

Jim gets to his feet and remains standing. He looks up at the top of the tree.

"Why does it hurt so much then, if it's all over?"

"I don't know."

"You have to face up to it, Lone. It's all or nothing."

"Have you forgotten she's your child too?"

"I'm sorry, Lone. Without you there is only night."

# FROM ETERNITY'S PERSPECTIVE
## (VITA)

It is the ocean of his childhood, the Atlantic. Vita beside him, in a soft summer scarf with fine golden threads.

"Jim, don't swim too far out, will you?"

A newspaper blows to and fro over the sand as she rolls over on the blanket and falls asleep. The beach empties of people. Jim walks back down to the water and resumes constructing a sandcastle; when the tide comes in he has to shift the structure further away. Time passes, the ocean's time. Every now and again he runs up to check that she is still asleep. Up above, the clouds scud past. A fighter plane climbs and dives, the smell of petrol and ash, a distant fire, blazing forests. When he comes back she is no longer there. A sudden solar eclipse, a black sun hanging over the sand dunes.

Jim thinks they should bury Vita in one of her spring coats, the pale blue one with mother-of-pearl buttons, the one she was dancing in on one of the last evenings she was up out of bed, before she departed. He was not in Stockholm when she died and when he returns, standing inside the door with his suitcases, the call comes from the head of the Royal Library where Vita has latterly been working.

"We don't usually make provision for the funeral of a suicide, in the way we normally do for our employees, but we'll make an exception if you would like her to have a ceremony.

Would you like that?"

"Is it possible to bury her in her spring coat?"

"I don't follow."

"Can we bury her in her pale blue coat?"

"As far as I'm concerned you can bury her in whatever you want. But first you must take a view on whether she is going to be buried at all."

"She'll be buried in her spring coat," Jim whispers into the warm telephone.

# THE ILLNESS

I have been asking for Jim everywhere, but no-one has seen him. Perhaps he has left the hospital. Edvard is missing too. They let me sit on the bench under the tree; sometimes Inger Vogel passes, often in a hurry now, sprinting under the lime trees. I ask if she wants to talk, and would she like to give me a menthol cigarette, but more often than not she has no time.

"Have you seen Jim?"

"He must be in his room."

"No, he isn't."

"Come back another day and you're sure to find him."

I lie on the bench and glimpse the sky peeping through the leaves, an unreal blue, unspeaking. The wind tugs at tiny pink blossoms in the trees. The heat makes me drowsy, like a fever.

One day, a man comes up to me. When he stands over me he is like a giant. Arctic blue eyes, blurred tattoos over his arms. He asks if I am waiting for someone, and could he wait with me, and before I can reply he sits down next to me.

"Are you waiting for your boyfriend?"

"I don't like boys," I say, as I lie there, squinting up at the sun.

He laughs and touches my fur coat on the bench.

"What do you like then?"

"Lying like this, falling asleep in the sun."

"That's nice. I do too."

I sit up and take a look at him. It is difficult to see his face in the bright sunshine, but I like his outline, his huge shadow on the grass.

"Why are you in here?"

"You don't want to know."

Much later I will get to know, but by then it will be too late. Or by then it will not matter, because he will already be a part of me.

"Or do you want to know?"

"I don't know. Do I?"

"Is it your dad you're waiting for?"

"Yes."

"Isn't he coming?"

"I don't think so. I don't think he wants to see me."

"Why?"

"It's something to do with my mum. I thought if I waited long enough he'd come out, but he hasn't."

"What's his name?"

"Jim."

He lets out a whistle.

"Jimmie Darling. They've moved him."

"Have they?"

"Yes. He's not here anymore. And I don't know where he is."

He takes a photograph out of his wallet and shows me a picture of himself and a little boy with blue eyes. The photograph is thumbed and faded, the colours washed out, as if he has looked at the picture so many times it is being dissolved by his eyes.

"Benny doesn't want to see me at all."

They all show me photographs of their children; whenever I talk to anyone for more than two minutes, out come the kids' photos. They all have the same smudged pictures in their wallets, no-one has any new pictures, and they are all so alike I sometimes think it is the same children, the same hopeful eyes staring into the light of the camera. Some of the photographs appear to be old, black and white with jagged edges. As if the pictures were proof of something. There is not much else to do, he says.

"With a child you're not under suspicion. With a child you're like everyone else. Even if it's only a worn old photo."

"Why doesn't he want to see you?"

"He doesn't think I was very nice to his mum."

"So, weren't you?"

He laughs and says he was nice sometimes and that he would like to meet me again. Through his open shirt I can make out the shape of an old woman, a pale tattoo that could almost be a shadow next to his heart. When he leaves I go back to sleep on the bench.

The window in Jim's room is banging in the wind, the impression of his body on the sheets as if on sand, but there is no-one in the room. I stand by the open window and watch a man

177

chase a woman over the lawn. There is something about the building, all perspectives collapse in here; at first I do not see that it is Edvard and her, I only see an unknown woman flouncing around in an open raincoat between the trees with a man after her. Then I recognise the big boots. No-one else would run outside in her underclothes except Sabina. When he catches up with her he grabs her necklace and rips it off her. For a moment it looks as though she is standing in blue rain.

The next time we see each other it is almost dark, the blue hour, and a slender moon hangs low in the sky. I do not know what he is doing outside so late; the surroundings are deserted as he comes walking towards me. I have forgotten how big he is, superhuman almost, he could so easily hurt someone, pick me up and carry me off if he tired of talking to me. Soon the sun will be gone.

"Do you live alone?"

"Of course I don't."

"Where's your mum then?"

"By the Black Sea."

"Isn't that a bit strange?"

"What?"

"That you're here on your own."

"I don't know. I didn't want to go."

"So who's looking after you now?"

"I'm looking after myself."

Lone thinks that she will not grow old if she flies all the time, that time will not catch up with her in the air. She knows nothing. Actually, people age more quickly in the air. The enormous pressure accelerates decline, and time goes faster in space. It is the same thing with angels, they live at top speed and are burnt out by the light. Valentina Tereshkova appeared to have aged twenty years when she returned from Vostok 6, she looked as though she had been away for decades. I tell him about it.

"I've never flown anywhere," he says, and at that moment we hear the sound of an aircraft as it rends the heavens above. Aeroplanes pass here all the time, sometimes so low they seem to touch the rooftops. As low as the clouds disintegrating when they bump into the hospital buildings, drifting on, damaged, deformed. Clouds and families, this is the place where all are sundered; the ponderous sky above where clouds get caught, line up, collide, before drawing apart to live on as half-clouds – orphaned, abandoned child-clouds.

The underbellies of the clouds are like gold this evening and he says he has to go, although he has just arrived, and I do not know where my entreaty comes from. Perhaps all words are supplications. Pleas and pearls. Sabina's pearls are lying in my pocket. I know now that his name is Paul, that he has been here several years already.

"Are you my friend?" I ask, fingering the broken necklace.

"If you want me to be your friend, I will be."

"Can you ask Jim to come down to see me?"

He takes my face between his hands. From his mouth comes a dull smell of earth and bad teeth.

"I have to go now."

"Stay with me awhile."

"You know how it is. I have to go back."

"And then?"

"I'm not like your dad. I'm more sick."

"What's he like, then?"

"He's a normal bloke with a job. This is just temporary for him. I've got nothing left out there; I'll never get out again."

When I look at him he turns his face aside, so I see the woman on his bare chest instead. She is trapped inside her own shadow there, listening to the beat of his heart. Paul pushes me away and gently presses me down onto the bench.

"You understand that this is wrong, don't you? That I'm here with you. Like this."

"I want you to come back," I say.

"You're a child. You have no idea what you want."

"I'll soon be fourteen. Will I know what I want when I'm forty-four?"

He laughs and I look at his pupils; they are different sizes. I had not noticed it before. One is gigantic and the other small as a pinhead. Darkness pours out of the large one, and perhaps the smaller one swallows up all the light, draws it in, captures it. No-one can live without light, and that might be why I like being with him, to feel I am in the light beside his darkness. It is measureless, his darkness; when I touch him the first time, my fingers in his hair, it feels as though I am touching the night, cool and clean under my hand, starlit.

"No. You'll know even less then. You'll know nothing at all."

Every day I find pearls in the grass outside the chapel, as if they multiply with time. I intend to give them back, but in the end I keep them. Twelve cornflower-blue pearls. Indigo, azure, sky, Prussian blue.

Edvard takes Jim and the others to Lake Judarn. They go by bus to Ekerö, through farmland and birch woods. Sabina accompanies Edvard in the car and Jim takes the bus with the others. While they sit on blankets by the black lake and lie outstretched on the jetties, dozing half the day, the sun slowly moves behind the ageing trees. Inger Vogel sits with her huge white ball of wool, stationed a little further up the beach, prepared to move in if needed, swatting at mosquitoes and giant flies. The water smells of death and lead; yellow seeds float languidly over the glassy, mirror-like surface, a hard, whisked-up foam quivering at the edge of the shore. A strip of land with coarse sand and patches of ragged leaves spread out like liver spots on the sludge. Sabina in a yellow bikini reflected in the oily, stagnant water. Edvard, glistening, close to her.

"The only thing I'm missing in hospital is the heavens," she says to him.

"Don't you see the heavens there?"

"I only see myself there."

"But maybe you've got them inside you?"

"The heavens?"

She gives a harsh laugh.

"If you knew what I had inside me, my dear Edvard, you wouldn't be sitting here."

Sabina swims out to the middle of the lake and Jim walks off along the muddy forest beach. He can hear their laughter over the water, the little group of bathing patients, so easily entertained and grateful, throwing themselves at a given signal into the black pool between the fir trees. Jim lies on the ground and shuts his eyes: a solitary bier floating in the sunlight, Vita in a shroud. He once stood beside that bier to say goodbye, and at the time she looked more like a photograph than a person; and when he bent to kiss her he was suddenly afraid and stopped. When he was close, the rose someone had placed at her breast stank of decay, of rancid rose oil and raw nature, and he felt as though it were reaching for him, as though something live was crawling over her dead body; the bacteria in the rose and the brown stuff of death assailing the edges of the leaves would soon destroy her too. Why is his dead mother floating here? A debt he does not know how he incurred, a woman who is here no longer and yet will not let him go. He wishes she would leave him in peace, as he does her. That night on the motorway, on his way to the airport, he has decided to destroy her. He swallows two hundred sleeping tablets but eliminates neither himself nor her; she is still inside him, like a face just under the water, pale as marble, her outline blurred. When he looks at himself in the lake's surface his face is replaced by hers, a shaky, slapdash watercolour. For the most part he sees dead women everywhere around him, lying outstretched under trees, naked or with their pants slipping down, their torn clothing contorting their arms and pinning them into grotesque shapes, in fields, on beaches, their hair the colour of rye, or black. They look as though they were trying to escape an invisible hunter, legs and arms at unnatural angles that make him think of raw chicken. Shadows of acts, of criminal love, the marks of red deer and roebuck covering their bodies.

On the way back to the group the large leaves strike against his face. Sabina is sitting on the jetty, wet and freezing, a cigarette drooping from her fingers, grey with cold and tiredness. Jim sits down beside her, takes the cigarette from her and lights it. Edvard is sitting further up the beach, watching them; he always does, like a mighty bird of prey he moves soundlessly above them, in the dormitories at night, in the showers, in the exercise yard, between the trunks of the birch trees in the copse on the other side of the fence.

# THE LAST PATIENT
# (STILL IN THE LIGHT)

"You do know Olof Palme's dead?"

Olof flinches as though someone has hit him. He hides his head in his hands, and whispers.

"Olof Palme's dead. Why do you say that?"

"Hasn't anyone told you?"

He shakes his head.

"No . . ."

"Olof Palme was assassinated ten years ago."

"No. No. No."

"I'm sorry, but it's true. Olof Palme has gone. A long time ago."

Olof looks up, his hands pressed against his cheeks.

"I understand. I simply haven't kept up. If Olof Palme's dead, there's no hope for the likes of me."

"Do you know he used to visit his mother when she was admitted here?"

"Did he?"

Olof lowers his hands and looks at Dr Janowski with big, tear-filled eyes.

"Yes. He visited her every morning on his way to the government offices in Rosenbad."

Olof rises from the chair and points a shaking finger out of the window.

"I thought I saw him here on several occasions. A long

time ago. But I always thought I was imagining it. I thought it was the hallucinations. More than once I saw him get out of a car outside Stora Kvinns. From my window. It was like a dream. That he had come here. I thought he'd come to fetch us. And once I saw Nelly Sachs in a pink coat outside here. As small as a doll . . . Was his mum sick?"

"Palme's mother? Yes, very. She didn't know who he was anymore, but she was always happy when she saw him."

Olof sinks down into the chair with a smile that illuminates from within.

"I can understand that. You're always so happy when a visitor comes. In the beginning Mum came. Then she stopped coming. An angel used to visit me after that. She even . . ."

"Yes?"

"Do you know something? Once she did it to me."

Dr Janowski laughs softly.

"That's great."

"Do you think so? I thought that maybe it was . . . inappropriate. With an angel."

"I think it sounds wonderful."

"I've never told anyone, but that's what happened. It was my first time, but it's ages since she came to me. She was fantastic. Without her I'd never have survived. I always hoped she didn't visit any of the others, but she wasn't the kind you could tie down."

INGER VOGEL

I did not recognise her at first, or her voice, but she said my name over and over again, quietly, tentatively, like before, though her voice was hoarser now, cracked.

"Jackie ... Jackie ... Jackie ..."

She was sitting in the sun on Odenplan Square with a carafe of wine in front of her and a black pup on her lap when Marion and I walked past on our way to Vasa Park. Her face was different, wider now and somehow set, but after a while she seemed to force herself slowly out of her strange new features, her eyes still green but lighter, like sea water. One narrow, squinting eye and one wide open; I concentrated on the wide-open eye, it seemed to belong better with the flat voice and the face she had now. The other eye belonged to another age and another woman, she who once walked around with a huge bunch of keys jangling at her hip and hands soft as lace.

She told me she had left Beckomberga just a few days before the hospital closed, that she had been one of the last to leave the building. Now she sometimes did night duty at St Göran Hospital, watching over patients who no longer wanted to live. Every fifteen minutes she had to go in and check they had not hanged themselves with their shoelaces. They were needing her less often, she said, so she was doing fewer and fewer hours.

"Maybe it's just as well. They don't want to live any longer after all," she said, looking at me with tired eyes, broken by alcohol and too much sun.

"Sometimes I think they should just be allowed to take themselves off, that I should look the other way for a moment and let them fly away. I sit watching them all night, but they have nothing to live for."

She did not ask about Jim, perhaps she thought he was dead.

"You're still as sweet as honey," was all she said, then lit a White Blend and inhaled so sharply it sounded as if something inside her was cracking.

"Drop in one night at St Göran if you like," she went on. "I'm usually in Ward 32, knitting. Not much happens there."

When I walked past a few hours later she was still sitting outside at the café, in the company of some elderly women now, and I do not think she saw me. She still had the black puppy on her lap. When I turned I could see her kissing the little creature over and over again.

Lone is calling to me from yet another dream I have this winter. She is in the hospital garden under a tree, looking lost, her handbag in her arms like a little dog.

"I was suddenly worried about you, Jackie."

"Were you?"

"Yes."

"Don't be. Marion and I are fine. You know that, don't you?"

She looks up at the tawny-red façade. A few winter birds are slowly circling round the clock tower.

"It seems as though they're finally pulling down the hospital and putting up houses," she says, a stroke of light in her voice.

"I know, though I wish they'd leave everything alone."

"But it would be awful to let this old mental hospital remain, wouldn't it? Why would they do a thing like that?"

"I don't know. Maybe because the building itself is a personification of sadness, of Jim's, of everyone's. A kind of recognition. Jim once said to me that coming here was like coming home."

"Did he really say that?"

The birds have gone now; it is utterly silent around us.

"Yes. He said this is a place that everyone dreams about coming to."

She turns and looks at me. The intensity in her eyes makes me almost back away. In the distance is the sound of an aeroplane taking off from the airport and darkness is rapidly falling around us, as if someone has thrown a blanket over the sun.

"And the man in the hospital?"

"Yes, what about him?"

"I've never liked to ask you about him."

"What do you want to know?"

"I'd like to know what it was like, what happened."

"Would you really?"

"Yes, I think so."

Lone looks away again, her eyes suddenly glassy.

"Did he hurt you?"

"No, he didn't, he helped me. Paul would have walked through fire for me."

# GRAVITY THE SEDUCER

Days pass. We meet under the tree, in the flickering shadow. No-one asks anymore what I am doing, who I am visiting. Paul walks around without his shirt, tending to the trees. I have never met anyone as calm as him, as straightforward, as present; a vein of cold still water runs through him. He says he will stay here forever. Perhaps he will; he has no desire to be elsewhere. We do not speak very much; we play chess and wait.

"Have you seen a bleeding-heart vine?" I ask.

"No."

"Nor me. If we meet somewhere else other than here we can try and track one down."

He laughs his big laugh with a flash of his bad teeth.

"Do you think we'll do that, Jackie?"

"Yes, I do."

Something brown has attacked his teeth and his saliva has a taste of iron and a strong taste of something else: decay, death, waste matter.

"Each time I hope it's the last time I see you."

"Why do you say that?" I ask.

"Because it feels like this is going to give me a seizure."

"This, with me? Honestly?"

"It feels as though everything inside me is bleeding."

The trees' roots look as though they have pushed up out of the ground and are lying like huge fingers resting in the grass. Paul's breaths are light as a butterfly, like a girl's, timid. He does not seem capable of harming anyone, and to me he is innocent, whatever he has done. He is no villain; he is too gentle for that. And he closes his eyes to the sun, as if he hopes that I will be gone when he opens them again. But I do not disappear, it is he who leaves me every time. In a few minutes he will be locked up in Stora Mans again. After a while he stands up and cautiously shakes my shoulders to wake me up.

"Please, don't wake me," I say.

"You can't fly around out here, little bumblebee. It's not going to end well, all this."

"Must it end?"

"I'll finish up in prison because of you."

I laugh.

"I thought you were already in prison."

The curator from the Natural History Museum is visiting again. He is walking briskly across the quadrangle. Under his arm is a thin briefcase that he never puts down when he is in the ward. Perhaps he thinks someone will want to steal it. His hurried manner down the corridors worries everyone seated there, making them withdraw into their rooms. Even Sabina becomes a different person when he is around. She moves slowly and quietly, as if someone has suddenly turned down her volume. A few hours later he storms back across the park.

*

When I come closer I see that she is weeping. The white scarf she has been knitting for so long is trailing on the ground, the fringe discoloured by mud. She turns away, dries her tears, and leaves streaks of mascara on her face. Dark moons under each eye. Behind her a pale sun is visible between the treetops, the birds singing in the distance, so few of them now and their sounds so feeble, but still their song comes through the trees. Where have all the other birds gone? Usually they fly back and forth over the fence that separates the hospital from the woods outside, from the rest of the world.

"Have you seen Jim?" I ask.

"No, he won't come back to me either."

I look at the skin on her pale hands, so thin the veins are like shadows, like entrails showing under the surface. A new piece of jewellery round her neck, a charm. She smells faintly of ether. A man I have never seen before is with her. It looks as though he is sleeping soundly in the sunshine. She has red marks on her shins and neck and is moving mechanically, as if someone has wound up the clockwork inside her, her movements wooden and jerky, perhaps the medication causing it, or her recent solitude. She has been in isolation for several weeks and this is the first time I have seen her since, sitting here on the grass, white as paper.

"It was like fighting with a big angel," she says. "I didn't stand a chance."

"Are you allowed out now?"

"Sometimes. Until I mess up again."

"Was it my fault?"

"How could it be your fault?"

"I don't know. I just thought it might be. All those packets I fetched for you."

"No way. Those silver packets saved my life."

She rises to her feet, looks as though she is freezing. I take off my fur and drape it carefully over her shoulders. She wraps it round herself and looks at me.

"What are you going to do now, Jackie?"

"I don't know," I say. "That's what I don't know."

"If you're in doubt, you have to do the brave thing."

I can see Paul's eyes in front of me, how he looks at me without averting his gaze, as if I were chosen, as if he would do anything for me, anything to protect me.

"Okay. But how do I know what the brave thing is?"

She presses her hand against my ribs, my heart thumps against her palm.

"You just will. You have this."

I was alone at home in the evenings; I stood in Lone's bedroom looking at my body in the mirror. A soiled vest and pants with no elastic. I used to hold them up with safety pins because I was so slim. No bra yet. The pointed ridges of my hips, the hair falling over my face. On the other side of the mirror the world was beginning.

Paul is on edge. He says he is sorry about it, he scratches his arms until there are huge weals and sometimes his whole body jerks uncontrollably. He weeps with his enormous hands pressed to his face. We are lying sprawled on a blanket at the edge of the hospital grounds, in the shade of the trees. I look at him as he gets to his feet, at the shadow that passes over his face, and when he unfolds his massive body he l ooks as though he belongs to another race, a different, giant breed. But his eyes are brimming over with love and light.

"Have you spoken to him?" I ask.

"Not yet."

"You have to. Soon. Today."

"I'll try. But I haven't seen him out for ages."

"Where have they moved him to?"

"No idea."

Under the gold inscription he tells me that his girlfriend became sick when Benny was born, that she went into a psychiatric clinic where she stayed for months.

"Wasn't she happy about the baby?"

"Yes, but she said she went to pieces because she felt safe with me at last."

"With you?"

"Yes, I think so."

Then he seems to change his mind.

"Maybe it was because of me she got sick, I just wanted to drink and sleep."

"And Benny?"

"She loved him like crazy. She'd never have left him of her own free will. The last night he was with me I held him in my arms until it was light. I sat absolutely still so I didn't wake him."

"And then?"

"Then they took him away."

We are lying on Lone's bed, talking and smoking and watching the smoke rise above our heads. Just under the ceiling it is broken up by the gentle movements of the suspended fan. It is warm from the sun streaming in through the open window and Paul is playing with my toes as I lie like a cross over the bed with my feet against his naked stomach. When he is allowed out, he comes to me. He has a few free hours in the week and has time to stay for forty minutes before he has to travel all the way back. He tells me he thinks of me all the time, that he sees my face in front of him when he falls asleep and when he wakes. I do not tell him I think about him; I do not tell the people I like anything, because I have no words. After a while he carefully undresses me, first my dress and then my pants. He kneels on the bedclothes and looks as though he is opening a fragile little parcel. I keep my vest on, I do not want to show him my breasts. His nipples look like sweets next to the tattoos, pale pink and covered in faint freckles, and when he takes off his jeans his penis stands in a curve in front of him. When he enters me he cries as if I have wounded him; but he has no need to be sad, I am ready for the pain, the flashing knife within me, and I like his body on top of me, the unreal light of his eyes that look at me afterwards.

"If love is insanity, we'll have to put it in isolation," he says. "You're the only one, Jackie."

If love is an illness, then Paul is the sickest person I have ever met and I am so afraid he will be cured.

"Don't be scared, baby," he says, as he clenches my hands above my head. "There's no way to get better from this."

The ceiling fan whirrs on its highest setting and the bed is in the shade now; we have fallen asleep and been woken by the telephone ringing. Perhaps it is Lone in a kiosk by the Black Sea, listening to muffled signals flowing from the black receiver. Paul hides his face in the pillow. Before he goes back to the hospital he comes into me again and this time there is no pain, only a pulse beating and beating inside me until everything suddenly tightens and then relaxes, and soon I am filled with an immense and remarkable light, a soothing, sun-warmed liquid released into my body, a sweet, blind carbonic acid. When we are at our closest, when his eyes are about to burst, he puts his hands round my neck, testing. A slight pressure on the bones and muscles holding my head up, a simple question.

"Jackie?"

I do not answer because I have nothing to say, because I do not know what kind of question it is, I only know that my vertebrae run like a thread inside in the darkness, a rosary in my body's loneliness, an absurd hope or a string of lights, of possible misfortunes. I think it must be love that is the true madness: passion, vertigo, hysteria.

I sit under the tree, waiting. Inger Vogel stands beside me, her shadow falling softly over the bench. She says nothing, lights a menthol cigarette, and blows out tiny smoke rings in front of her. The smoke is cool and clean and thinner than normal, and she stands there next to me looking across Clock-House Park with a little circle of smoke floating over her head. As if she wants to be close to me, as if she wants to protect me from something, but she knows not what.

# FROM ETERNITY'S PERSPECTIVE
## (VITA)

She is in front of him, wearing a glistening white bathing costume. Her hair is still wet and lies twisted in a coil over her breast. They are standing by the English Channel in the blinding white sea light of his childhood, where once they spent their summers. Jim is holding a cuttlefish almost as big as himself, he can hardly get his arms around it; its dead body is cold and slimy against his chest and its eyes are gigantic, unmoving mirrors.

"Jimmie," she says, taking his hand, "can't you just come back with me?"

"I can't, Mother, I have to stay here for a bit."

"But there's nothing left here. And the water's perfectly gentle out there, it's not dangerous."

She looks at him from behind her sunglasses and her voice sounds as it always has, warm and softly lulling. Seaweed and bladderwrack have fastened to her bathing costume and when she takes his hand in hers, cold and pale, with the veins glinting under the skin on her wrists, he quickly pulls away.

"I'll come later. Soon."

# THE OBSERVATORY

*The Goldilocks Zone is an astronomical term for a point in the universe where life can arise. A planet must be at exactly the right distance from a star in order not to be burnt away by the light or frozen solid.*

"You've always liked trees," Lone says, standing a short distance away in the park. It is late winter now and in Clock-House Park the trees have been bare and lifeless for a long time; they look as though they will never manage to bear leaves again. Darkness falls rapidly now; it is harder and harder to summon up these dreams.

"Yes, I have," I say.

"Why?"

"Maybe it's the way they reach out for light and water. Because they look as though they're in prayer when they bend their tender trunks over the river."

"But who can comfort a tree?"

"The spring perhaps, the first light. When I was little I always thought trees pretended to be dead in winter."

Lone glances up at me with her beautiful large eyes.

"That's like Jim. He goes under and then rises up again in spring."

When I do not reply she reaches out her hand to me and I hold it in mine. It is quite cold, chilled through and small, almost like Marion's.

"Are you sad, Jackie?"

"No, not anymore."

"When did you stop being sad?"

"Maybe it was when Marion arrived. Maybe it was because he was a boy."

Her eyes are wide open, utterly clear and pure, as if she has just washed them.

"Because he was a boy?"

"Yes, because he isn't me. I can't explain it."

"You don't have to explain anything to me, Jackie. I think I understand anyway."

"Do you?"

"Yes. Or I wouldn't be here."

When I was a child, before I began going to school, I looked at Jim one day and realised he did not see the pale green trees that swayed above us. I have always loved their enormous crowns and roots, believing that the delicate light they let through their leaves for humans has protected me from danger.

He was standing next to me and I touched his hand.

"Can't you see the trees, Jim?"

"What trees?"

"The birch trees, the pines, I don't know, the big oak trees over there."

But he really did not see them. Everything passed him by. He stood there, smoking his cigarettes and listening to Vita's voice inside him; I could never drown it out.

I used to play in Observatorielunden Park while he lay sleeping it off in the shade. He lay on the grass curled into a foetal position and it looked as though he was having nightmares, as if something was chasing him in his dreams. The large trees kept us safe as they let the world's light fall over his sleeping figure. Sometimes we went into the Observatory and looked at the stars through a huge telescope; it seemed as though the whole sky were suddenly in the room with us, that we had left the earth behind. Absorbed in the firmament, it did not matter who we were, that Lone had gone away again, that we were alone in the city, he and I, that he was drinking all the time from a little bottle he kept at the bottom of his sports bag. The atmosphere seemed made of fragile layers, faintly afloat, and behind it – eternity and the stars. I assume he got drunk because he needed to, and when we stood in the Observatory it was as if we were the only living people left on earth. He said that one day my star would fall to me from the heavens and everything I wished for would be mine.

"Be careful what you wish for now. Everything comes true."

One night, just after I was born, Jim and Lone planted a little tree in Observatorielunden Park. The baby tree, they called it, and then the girl tree, and every birthday through my childhood we sat under that small silver willow among the mighty oaks and ate sandwiches and cake. When Jim left us we stopped going there together and I went by myself.

Jim had girlfriends and casual lovers all over, with names that sounded like tourist destinations or drugs: Nanna, Jo, Katt, Oline, and in the evenings he was drawn towards the light of the bars by Tegnérlunden Park. More often than not Lone and I were by ourselves in the apartment while the sun made its way in an arc from the whiteness of the bedroom, over the flock wallpaper of the living room, before slowly drenching the tiny kitchen in a soft orange glow. Now and then Jim bounced in, wearing his big white sheepskin coat and bearing sweet wine and gifts: a cheese that Lone loved, an encyclopaedia of which every page seemed dipped in gold, a toy I was in fact too big for. Then he was gone again for days, sometimes for weeks. Lone did not hear from him, she rang around asking after him, and every so often we would find ourselves in a strange hallway waiting for Jim to get dressed and come home with us.

---

Lone spreads out a blanket on the grass and then we drink a toast to me in the shade of my birth tree. I am nine, ten, eleven in the autumn. The tree is full-grown now, standing among other trees like a dark, aged hand. Jim's eyes are brimming with a low, devouring light; inside him is the precipice that makes him so restless, that makes him want to leave as soon as he has settled down and rush off along the street. But Lone persuades him to lie still a moment longer and close his eyes against the sun. Lone's voice next to his heart, her high brow, the pale red hair cascading down her back.

"Stay with me a little while, Jim."

But Jim drinks more and more, and the alcohol changes character now; the blood in his veins flows more sluggishly, there is no light about him, just an irritated listless flicker, an oversensitivity and constant nervousness that pricks beneath his skin. His brief glimmers of clarity are increasingly rare, receding ever further. Now and then in the bathroom mirror he glimpses a black sun.

Edvard passes a packet of cigarettes over the table. Sitting with his hands hidden in the sleeves of his sweater, Jim shakes his head. A brief flare of a match and then the cold smell of smoke. Dim institutional lights, the low buzzing of electricity around them.

"I don't think you're one of them, Jim."

"One of whom?"

"Suicides. And I don't think you'll succeed."

"Don't you?"

"The healthy part of a person runs side by side with the sick, two wells or veins impossible to separate. Being sick can also mean taking responsibility, protecting your immediate surroundings from a rage that threatens to destroy everything."

Edvard lets a trail of smoke slowly out of his mouth before he continues.

"If you say that you're standing in a circle, I'll say I don't believe in circles."

"And what happens to the circles then?"

"Nothing at all."

"Nothing?"

"If you're not free now, Jim, you'll never be free."

Jim is in the exercise yard when Paul comes up. Around them people move like shadows, old men in baggy hospital trousers and jackets. Above them hovers a cloud of cigarette smoke. Grainy morning light, yellowish, like fever. Jim is thin, leaner, his legs slender in his jeans, and he is slightly suntanned. The sun always finds him, wherever he is, even when he keeps to the shade; there is a special sun that shines on him, a scorching light of doom that makes his skin brown and smooth.

"Someone said you'd left," he says when he sees Paul.

"Everyone's always saying everyone else has left. But no-one leaves here."

"I'm starting work in August."

"Right."

"I'll be quite careful at first. Nothing much, just go and sit in the office. When I came here I thought I'd only be in for a few days."

Paul laughs his short, tinny laugh.

"Everyone thinks that. Everyone thinks they're in the wrong place. It passes. Then you don't want to get out."

"Don't you wish you were away from here?"

"No, I don't. There's nothing left out there."

"Surely everything's there."

"Not for me. Not for most of us."

"But there's nothing here."

"There's everything. It's like a small town. And it doesn't matter where you are. You can't escape from yourself."

Paul looks at him until he finally averts his gaze.

"Your daughter's special."

"Is she?"

"Haven't you noticed?"

"It's a long time since I saw her."

"She's been here, asking for you. She usually sits and waits under the tree over there. I talk to her sometimes."

A faint breeze tugs at the tops of the trees above. Paul touches his shoulder.

"Haven't you seen her sitting there? Why don't you just come down?"

"I don't know. I don't know what she wants. Not that I'd be able to give it to her anyway."

"If Benny came, I'd be so bloody happy. But he just sits and waits for his mum to come back. That's all he wants. Her. He doesn't want anything else. No presents, no telephone calls, nothing."

Jim laughs softly.

"They all want what they haven't got."

"They do, don't they? Forever something else. Benny was always so worried one of us would clear off. *What are you going to do when I've fallen asleep? When are you coming home again? Which way are you going to work?* And Marie sat there on the edge of his bed like a bloody angel and promised she would never leave him. I saw her sitting there in the circle of light from his night lamp, kind of lit up from inside herself. He always wanted it on, so that little lamp had to burn all night. In the morning he stood looking at us until we woke up. He never woke us, just stood there watching, as if he was guarding us."

"And it all turned to shit anyway?"

Paul nods slowly.

"It always does. There's no point being afraid of happiness, it doesn't last long in any case."

"I've never been as happy as I've been here. At the hospital. Isn't that strange?"

"Not particularly."

"Why should I be happy here?"

"I don't know. I just don't think it's strange."

"Maybe not. When did you last meet him? Your boy."

"A long time ago. The last time was straight afterwards. I was allowed in for a bit, I think I got thirty minutes. I wanted to give him everything, and all I got was thirty minutes. I'd already decided I was going to tell him myself. It was the only thing I could do for him, to tell him exactly what happened, not to lie, not to leave anything out."

"What did you tell him?"

"I told him like it was. I said that in the seconds before I did it, I had no thought of hurting her. I said it was so easy to kill her, so much easier than I could have imagined. That she was just soft in my hands, like always. One breath away and she wasn't mine any longer. Everything we had between us was over in an instant."

"Did you tell him like that? Your boy. Like you told me just now?"

"Yes. It was different, though. He didn't want to hear. He tried to run away. So I'm writing to him now. I think it's good for him. To know, to understand what love can be like, that it can exist in hell as well. And I knew something that she didn't, about love. Something she never felt, was never anywhere near. It's the only thing I can do for him, but he doesn't want that either."

"I can't imagine you doing something like that," Jim says.

Inger Vogel stands by the entrance to Stora Mans and shouts. Paul starts to move, flings away the burning cigarette.

"Nor me. You never can. Her death is like an old nightmare about someone else. I'm only saying I think you should meet your daughter and not let her sit there waiting like a little monkey."

"Wait," Jim says hurriedly, standing up too, "tell me about Jackie. Is she alright?"

Paul does not reply.

"What's she doing?"

"She's waiting for you, for you to come down to her. And she's in love."

"How beautiful. In love."

"I don't know if it's so beautiful."

"Isn't it?"

"No, it's not beautiful."

Jim and Lone are in the kitchen on Kammakargatan, in the last of the afternoon light, she with a blue bowl and a whisk in her arms, making one of her lemon tarts, he with a glass of sherry in his hand.

"I'll put my head in the oven so you know where I am," he whispers, kissing her neck.

When I am older it is Lone who keeps disappearing. She travels further and further away, wandering the other side of the world, where she photographs the devastation in disasters' wake, children running in poisonous rain, fallen trees, dead rivers. The Adriatic Sea. The Dead Sea. The Atlantic. The Indian Ocean. And while Lone is away everything falls into disrepair. Without her, things break and we do not know how to fix them. In the evenings I sit and try to do some stitching, holes in socks and shirts, mend the yellow dress I grew out of long ago. Everything is dirty and soiled, we wade through piles of clothes and other things lying on the floor and we dig out little channels to pick our way around. And when the light bulbs go, they go forever. Jim lies on the pull-out sofa with a brown beer bottle beside him, tapping on the table with the bottle top, and does not answer when I talk to him. When I ask about Lone, he turns to the wall. After a few days he gets up. He goes down to the off-licence on Tegnérgatan and from there to Observatorielunden Park, where he sits all day, talking to the dead. Sometimes it feels as though I could reach that place inside him.

<hr />

Jim used to sit in a restaurant on the opposite side of the street after work, and then at midnight he would go up to the office and clock out before reeling home to us. No-one ever asked him about those midnight hours, no-one ever said anything when he fell asleep in the coffee room. When he awoke, they had all gone. It was completely quiet, just the fluorescent light crackling above him and his spilt coffee on the table. It was as if he were in no-man's-land, as if he could do whatever he liked, as if he were immortal. He existed in the magic Goldilocks Zone that love forms for alcohol.

*Jim: It was a case of ensuring at all times that you were at exactly the right distance between life and death, so far from life that you begin to resemble a dead person, so close to death that you feel the chill liquid of fear down your spine, long moments submerged in oblivion or exposed to mortal danger. I fell in front of passing cars, I got in a hot-air balloon when I was drunk, I took so many tablets I stayed in a lift for a whole afternoon. Everything I did related to death, but I made sure that I was still at just the right distance from it. Deep inside my drunkenness I counted the hours until the doctor's appointment the following day. There was a doctor who prescribed sleeping pills and monitored my internal organs so they did not fail. There were several doctors, I had one in every part of town and one of them checked my levels every six months. Loss of control is just an illusion; in the depths of alcohol there is utter control. A cold and simple mathematics: I counted the damage, I tried to estimate its scope. And I never lied to you and Lone when I said I was in control. Only an alcoholic knows that control is total, it overshadows everything; I knew exactly when I had to stop drinking to be able to get myself out of bed and shuffle down Kammakargatan to the office, I knew when I had to cut out the drink. When I was carried up the stairs by some of my workmates after a meal, I knew exactly what I was doing. It was my protest, my rebellion.*

We went out in the car together when Lone was back and Jim had not yet taken off into the city. On those afternoons I lay in the back, enveloped in a cloud of smoke and voices, looking out at the serpentine road winding its way like a grey ribbon across the landscape. Lone sat at the wheel in her big sunglasses with Jim by her side, gazing at her. It was as if he could not see enough of her, he was staring all the time. But he had no idea how to care for her, how to keep her. Lone looked at the road stretching out in front of us, concentrating as always on the motorway and the large map open on her knee.

"I'm sorry I can't make us happy," Jim said, apropos of nothing. It was the soft, fuzzy afternoon light, before the night, and for a second he met my eye in the rear-view mirror and smiled the smile that always died as soon as he looked away. For a long time Lone sat quietly, as if she were thinking about what happiness was, and then she smiled and reached out her hand to him.

"I know you're sad. I am too. We'll get over this."

*Jim: At the end Lone and I would sit together on the sofa, both with a book, two identical smoke rings rising to the ceiling. The book I held in my hand was like a coffin; I had dreamed of writing, I had dreamed of playing the piano, but all my dreams were empty now. I walked to work in the mornings in a grey coat with a grey briefcase like hundreds of thousands of other men in the city every morning. At dusk I walked back up the hill to Kammakargatan and sat on the sofa with Lone. We looked out over the trees and the mist and the birds flying between the branches, and all the time I had a feeling that my organs were lying strewn out over the city. Lungs, kidneys, liver, gall bladder and heart, easy prey for the city's rats and birds.*

I am woken by Lone looking at me. It is light in the room. She must have come in during the night without my hearing her. I sleep with the door open in case Paul should turn up, but he no longer does. She is sitting on the edge of the bed. Her face is

223

suntanned and open, and she has brought with her the scent of wind and scorched grass. She has flown through the night to come home to me. A smell of ammonia from the sheets hits us when she carefully draws up the blanket. I have been sleeping in a puddle of urine.

"I think I've wet myself," I say, looking up at her.

"What a good thing I'm here," she whispers.

"Will you stay with me now, Lone?"

"Yes, I'll stay with you now."

Her eyes glaze over for a second, then she lifts me up in her arms and carries me into the bathroom.

"Did you go to Chernobyl?" I ask when I am sitting in the bath, letting her wash my back with a sponge. I suddenly remember it is covered in scratches from my shoulder blades down, but Lone just washes carefully around the weals, her hands gentle. It stings, as if she were washing me with fire, and I think Edvard is wrong, that it is not possible to fall without hurting yourself.

"No, I didn't," she says slowly. "I came home instead."

"How was Odessa then?"

I hear her tears behind me.

"It was awful."

# THE LAST PATIENT
## (STILL IN THE LIGHT)

Dr Janowski folds the hospital record carefully, smoothing it with his hand several times before he puts it to one side.

"What are you thinking about, Olof?"

Olof looks up and grips his little case harder.

"I'm thinking it's time to go now."

"Anything else?"

"I'm thinking about what was. Sometimes it felt as though this building was meant just for me, for me, alone in the world, that the locked room floated on its own in the universe when I was in the isolation ward."

"But you weren't alone. There were thousands of you."

"Yes, there were."

Dr Janowski stands up and positions himself by the window with his back to the sunset, so that his face is in shadow. A flock of jackdaws flies low over Clock-House Park, so low they look as though they will fly into the building opposite. At the last second, in electrifying unison, they swoop swiftly upwards. This room is all there is in the world now, the low buzzing noise that emanates from the fluorescent light, and Dr Janowski's voice.

"What do you see when you see yourself out there, free?"

Olof is silent for a moment, rubbing the palms of his dry hands together with small, rapid movements, as if to calm himself.

"Do you want to know what I see?"

"Yes."

"Well. It's winter. There's ice on the bay at Nybroviken. Huge snow flakes and bitter cold. People hurrying along the streets. Children skating in Kungsträdgården Park. A little ice rink lit up with lanterns. There's faint music from the loudspeakers."

He falls silent, looking down.

"And what about you, Olof, where are you?"

His hands are on his knees as the tears fall onto them.

"I'm lying huddled up on Hamngatan outside the NK department store in my winter coat. Above me people are hurtling by. I see them rushing past me, it's all so fast, like a jet plane. I'm so scared, Doctor."

"Where do you think they're going, all those people?"

"They're on their way into the future. And there's nothing there for me."

# THE AGE OF ANGELS

The trees have lost their leaves, bare, black, wet trunks, a low, milk-white sky without birds. I sit on the bench, waiting, as Jim comes sauntering across the quadrangle. A last butterfly flits over the grass, its wings seem too heavy for flight. A man rakes leaves nearby. Jim stands for a long time and does not speak, fiddling with an envelope in his hand.

"Hello, Jim."

"I've missed you, Jackie."

"Have you?"

"Yes."

"I thought you didn't want me to come again."

The butterfly, weighed down by its mighty wings, is quite still now. The colour of charcoal, the colour of earth, as if it were born in the soil from a chrysalis tomb.

"What have you missed, then?" I ask, when he says nothing.

He laughs and pokes the brim of my hat so it slips over my eyes.

"That hat. I've missed that hat."

We sit in silence for a while. I think how easy it would be to catch the butterfly and crush it in my hand, but I leave it alone. Jim looks different, not as haunted as before. He tells me he has had leave for a few days and been to the island of Stora Karlsö, off the coast of Gotland.

231

"I'll be leaving here soon."

"When's soon?"

"I don't know. I'm waiting for Edvard to say the word."

A brief shadow over the grass as a bird flies low across the sky. It must be a bird of prey; I follow it with my eye until it disappears into the white. I do not know what to say. I thought he would stay here forever. I thought this was the end of something, that he would never come back.

"So, are you better now?"

"I'll never be well, but I don't need to be in here anymore."

The butterfly raises its wings and flies a short distance across the grass before abruptly sinking to the ground, where it remains.

Sabina is waiting for Jim with a chessboard in her arms. She is wearing a black swimming costume under the fur coat, and Edvard's big wellingtons. She delves in her handbag and retrieves a lipstick, which she opens and then holds without using.

"You came back," she says.

"Of course I came back."

"I thought you'd gone for good."

She sets out the pieces in silence. They start the game and play at breakneck speed with great concentration.

"Do you think we'll see each other out there?"

"Definitely."

Sabina pauses. Then she carries on.

"So it was me who was attached to you in the end, and not the other way round. It's always that way. To begin with it's me who decides. Then I lose everything. Or I lose myself. I think you'll forget me the minute you walk through the gates."

"It would be very hard to forget you, Sabina."

"And if I stay here?"

"Then I'll come and get you."

They play on in silence.

"How do you imagine your own death, Jim?"

"Is that really the only thing you think about?"

"Not the only thing. I think about us as well. I think a lot about us."

Jim has permission to leave the hospital for a period every day and we go further afield, to where the lake is flooding its banks. The cold water has been rising for several weeks, pushing deeper into the woods. The water's temperature is near freezing even though it is summer water, icy and clear as glass. Later it will turn brown and oily, a heavy smell of sulphur and old rain hanging over everything.

"So you've met Paul?" he asks, sitting with a stone in his hand, looking out over the graphite gold of the lake.

"Yes," I say. "I usually help him with the garden behind Stora Mans."

Jim makes a gesture with his hand.

"What a fate. For a man as nice as Paul."

"What fate?"

"Don't you know?"

A flare of jagged flame inside me, a sudden heat surging through my veins.

"I don't think so."

The words recede, and reappear. Jim's voice is quick and light, as if relating something fantastic. On the other side of the lake the last of the sunlight filters through the drooping trees. Trees that are always drawn to water. From a distance it looks as though they have been trying to flee down to the lake from a hunter, been frozen mid-flight, heads bowed, branches overcome, lifeless and exposed. I close my eyes and feel Paul's large hands round my neck again, gauging, his warm breath against my hair, a simple question in the darkness.

"And Benny?" I ask, finally.

"They took him away."

"How do you mean?"

"They came and got him."

He throws the stone and divides the flat, blank surface. A thousand circles grow out of the point where it has disappeared.

Sabina's jumper smells of fire and forest. I press it against my face and let her hold me for a moment. Her breathing is slow and calm, and I wish I could stay here forever, next to her. Jim has gone back to the ward.

"Never mind, Jackie. Everything has its own time. The age of gold. The age of heroes. The age of angels."

"Do you think so?" I say, holding her harder. She is so slender beneath my hands, just ribs and heart. I am freezing in my cardigan; winter is on its way, a wave of cold and smoke permeating the air, the smell of newly fallen snow.

"You've already overtaken Jim," she whispers.

"Have I?"

"Yes, a long time ago."

"And Lone?"

"I don't know Lone, but no-one can ever overtake a mother."

Sabina has never spoken of her mother, I have assumed she only has the curator at the Natural History Museum, who appears from time to time in his suit and shuts himself in the room with Sabina. He fills the ward with his ill-tempered presence and no-one dares go near Sabina when he is around. Not even Edvard or Jim.

"You get sick," she says, "someone looks after you, you slowly change into a person you never thought you would be. And in the midst of the darkness is your mother."

Before we part by the gatehouse, she does up all the silver buttons on my cardigan. She gazes at me for a long time before gently pushing me away.

I sit curled up in the hospital bed next to Jim in the dormitory.

Our feet touch under the blanket, I have pulled my knees up so I can feel the soles of his bare feet against mine.

"You look different, Jackie."

"Do I?"

"More grown up. A miniature little woman."

"I've had my birthday."

"I know. Fourteen. The time of world domination. Tomorrow I'm leaving here. Did I tell you?"

"Yes, you told me."

"I think I missed summer. I'm sorry."

"I know, but it doesn't matter. There'll be other summers. Shall I come tomorrow?"

"No, don't do that. I have to do the last bit myself."

We sit in silence. Motes of dust float in the pale sunlight.

"Maybe I'll go to school tomorrow then," I say finally.

"Has it started now?"

"It started a few weeks ago."

He gives me a look that is absolutely clear, like a glass of water.

"Of course you must go to school. You're the future. Have you forgotten?"

"You once told me that this was the end of the future," I say, wriggling out of the bed. I walk over to the window.

"Did I say that?"

"Yes."

Jim's voice is calm and warm.

"I must have been talking about myself. You know, the first time I saw you in Lone's arms in the maternity hospital,

I thought, it's your world out there. I thought, this girl can do whatever she wants."

—∞∞∞—

I see Paul from a distance. He is outside Stora Mans with a case in his hand. A little further away is a black car, sinister and dark, with reflective mirrored windows. When I call he does not answer, his back rigid, stiff with anger. Only when I am right next to him does he look up and the cold glint around him vanishes. For a second our eyes meet, his pale eyes of unreal blue that pin me to myself. I try to win time as I can see he is about to go. I do not know how I will manage without him, there will be no-one after him. So I say it as it is, that he is still the person closest to me.

"That's fine, but I'll soon be far away from here," he answers, his eyes glistening.

"Where are you going?"

"I don't know. They're moving me."

The light is cold, ominous, deathly; I have not noticed it before, yellow and grainy over the bare trees. Volumes of water transform the hospital park into a fiery, ravenous river, engulfing the plain outside and leaving a trail of tangled saplings ripped out with their roots. The odour of graves hangs over the area, clouds the colour of bile, torn, sick shreds. Solitary stars begin appearing in the sky. My eyes fill with tears and the stars merge into one another, the sky a single milk-white film.

"Can I see you again?"

"I don't think so."

"You said you were my friend. Don't you remember?" He looks at me for a long time and then smiles his big beaming smile, opens the palm of his hand and blows onto it.

"Farewell little butterfly. Fly away now."

He turns and walks over to the car, throws his case into the boot and folds his huge body into the back seat. I see it happen and I cannot move, I cannot run, though I should rush at the car and stop him. There is something inside me that holds me back.

When I look up at the front of the building, Edvard is standing at a window, wearing dark sunglasses, watching me with his hands behind his back. He raises his hand and waves to me before vanishing into the darkness.

# FROM ETERNITY'S PERSPECTIVE
## (VITA)

"Which arrow flies forever, Jim?"

The trees' enormous crowns shield them from the intense sunlight. Jim practises with his bow and arrow on a board nailed to a tree trunk while Vita lies on her coat on the scorched grass, reading the newspaper. From the back she looks like a young girl, a skinny red belt around her waist, a headscarf for the sun, her thin legs bouncing restlessly up and down on the grass. A stranger seeing them now would never guess she is the mother of the young man with the bow in his hand, he could easily be her lover. When his arrow leaves the bow she turns away from the newspaper to see if it will hit its target, and for one amazingly protracted moment time slackens and the arrow makes an arc in slow motion through the air, and she looks at him as if he were holding it all in his hand, the forest, the future, and the arrow's course.

"Why did you give me the name James?"

Her eyes are bright and focussed and nothing could make her doubt him just now, her son and archer, the light in her night.

"Because it means 'he who may protect'. It was the most beautiful name I could give a boy."

"But who should I protect?"

"I don't know ... Yourself ... Your children ... Your daughter."

"But I've failed with all of that."

When the arrow finally hits the board with a crack, it is a bullseye. She winks at him and calls, "It doesn't matter, I failed as well. But for you there's still time. Have you forgotten?"

And with that she is gone.

# THE GRAVITY OF LOVE

On the way home from the hospital it rains, a soft warm rain. I peer in through the window of the shop with all the old paraphernalia. The man is asleep in the armchair with a giant stuffed crow on his lap; when I knock on the window he leaps up and comes out, the crow's claws resting on his enormous stomach.

"What have you done with that amazing cat?"

"I gave it away."

"That's good, you should always give your best things away."

"My dad's coming home tomorrow."

His eyebrows shoot up to his hairline.

"What a surprise! What a party you'll have. That's made me happy."

He looks down at the crow.

"Do you think he'd like to have this little bird? She comes from Berlin Zoo."

I cautiously stroke the stiff grey wings.

"Thanks, but I think he'll be okay."

He holds it tighter, as if suddenly regretting his offer.

"Yes, he probably will. I'm actually wondering whether to take it home myself."

"Where do you live?"

He looks surprised I do not know where he lives.

"I live here, of course."

He points to the curtain at the back of the shop. Then he kisses my cheek and reiterates how happy he is. As I walk away he calls after me.

"When we were kids we called girls crows."

I sit by the window in the stairwell, smoking a Hobson and staring out at the yard. A stray dog rummages behind the bins, looking for something to eat. It is so thin its ribs show under its fur. Lone meets me in the hall; maybe she heard me come through the door and has been waiting for me. I let her dry my rain-soaked hair with a pink towel. I gaze at her, I can never tire of looking at her.

"Lone, really, why did you come back?" I ask, when I am sitting on the sofa, naked from the waist up, raindrops on my cheeks. She stops what she is doing and lets the towel fall; she brushes some of the water off my forehead.

"I was frightened."

"What were you frightened of?"

"I was frightened something would happen to you. I woke up one night in Odessa convinced you were in danger. Were you?"

The rain is like a transparent wall outside. Late summer rain. I think of Sabina sitting on the slope under the birch trees, counting her pearls after the evening meal. I suppose she and all the others have already forgotten me, in the way people always forget those who have left the hospital.

"Jim's leaving Beckomberga tomorrow," I say, instead of answering the question.

"I know. He rang just before you got back."

"Will he come back to us then?"

Lone looks suddenly tired, as if she has not slept for weeks.

"You know he won't."

<hr />

The shop on Drottninggatan has been gone a long time. It is a coffee place now, with crystal chandeliers on the ceiling and golden angels on the walls. I was there with Rickard once, when I was pregnant with Marion, right at the start; I had just begun to feel those first spider-like movements inside me. It was as if someone had suddenly and swiftly flicked a feather through my stomach. Under the massive crystal chandeliers, I told him about the man and his shop full of old things, about the foxes and mannequins and hats.

"He vanished with a world that no longer exists. A world that was here when I was a child. Sometimes I miss it."

Then I told him about Beckomberga, which I had not done before. I told him about Sabina and Paul and Edvard and Jimmie Darling. When I fell silent he looked at me and said he wished he had known me as a child.

"What would you have done if you'd met me then?" I said.

"I'd have lifted you up and carried you away."

"But I wanted to be there. That was all I wanted."

"That's possible. I'd have done it anyway."

Jim sits in Edvard's room under the clock for the last time, blowing smoke rings over piles of medical records. The lamps above glimmer, a subdued, muted light. The curtain is drawn aside today and all the things you could stand contemplating for hours are visible: the skeleton, the skulls, the jars of formaldehyde. The sad old octopus floating in its watery grey light.

"Now then, Jimmie Darling. How does it feel?"

"I don't know. Good, maybe."

"Is anyone coming to collect you?"

"No, I'll take the bus."

"If not, there's the possibility of a taxi paid for by the hospital."

"No, I've longed to be on that bus."

"That's grand."

"You know, Edvard, I find it harder and harder to say goodbye. With every year that passes, farewells get worse. Now I can hardly get on a bus, because I'll have to part from the other passengers when I get off."

Edvard laughs and leans back in his chair.

"Isn't that Don Juan's dilemma?"

"What dilemma?"

"That he can't go without touching her."

"Probably. Will you look after Sabina?"

"You know I will."

"She needs something, only I don't know what it is. I can't

give it to her. Someone has to look after her."

Edvard gives him a hurried embrace.

"Only thinking about yourself can protect you to a certain extent, Jimmie, but in the end you'll have to start loving in order not to be ill again."

Jim goes down the stairs and leaves the hospital without turning around. At the gatehouse he lights a cigarette and takes a few quick drags before walking over to the bus stop.

We sat in Spökparken a few days later and watched darkness fall, quickly, as it does in autumn. I had received a thin silver chain and an amber comb as a birthday present. "Gifts from Sabina," Jim said.

He had telephoned and said he would like to celebrate my birthday in Observatorielunden Park, like before.

"How's Sabina?" I asked, pulling the gleaming, gold-coloured comb through my hair.

"Same as ever. Sad. A Sabina affliction."

"And you?"

"I'm fine. Life is a work of grief."

He had brought with him an old hammock from the shop on Drottninggatan, and we sat in it, suspended between heaven and earth. Night-time in the park has always arrived suddenly, as if someone were turning off a switch up above. We sat in the half-light and the only thing moving was his cigarette, hovering in front of us, a solitary firefly in the night. I had thought I would never ask, but every word is in reality a plea, and in the end inevitable. He gazed at me with his blue eyes, a blue so intense it turned into something else, into black; and the lonely look in his large, wandering eye, the iris around the fixed, hard pupil, threatening all the time to suck me in, was magnetic; it was so jaded, so blue, as if alcohol permeated the eye's fluid, aquavit blue.

"One night I dreamt you'd stopped drinking. I've always thought I couldn't imagine you sober, but in the dream I could. It was as if you'd never been any other way."

"What was I like then?"

"Different. Smooth. It was completely smooth in the dream. As if nothing had any edges."

Jim looked at me as if he were in another world, and then went on staring out over the park and at the darkness slowly descending over the silvery city.

"I'll never be able to give you that. It's the one thing I'll never be able to give you."


And when the spiders started crawling all over his chest that night on Observatoriegatan, I held him; I saw them coming before he discovered they were there.

"But you shouldn't be able to see them, it shouldn't be possible," he mumbled next to me, groping for my hands. It was true, I ought not to have been able to see his nightmares, but I have always seen them: primordial spiders springing to life out of the brandy, falling one by one from the ceiling onto his body with a soft electric sound, their creeping black bodies suddenly all over the bed.

An ocean bird flies slowly through the hospital at dusk. It is so pale it looks almost illuminated from within, and I catch only a brief glimpse as it glides along the corridors, then it is gone.

# WINTER IN STOCKHOLM

Edvard could not let go either, after Jim had left the hospital. A few weeks after Jim was discharged, Edvard telephoned to ask how things were going.

"How are you, Jimmie?" he asked.

"I miss everyone," Jim said, sitting by the window, staring out over Observatorielunden Park. Sabina lay in the bed, watching him; she was out for a few hours again.

"We miss you too. You can come tonight, if you'd like to. I'll invite you for a drink at Lill-Jans Plan at midnight. Come on."

So Jim and Sabina took a taxi, which Edvard came down and paid for. Then they sat on the little balcony on Lill-Jans Plan until dawn, wrapped up in thick blankets, looking out over the city. Winter was on its way; large snow clouds were rolling in from the east.

*Jim: I had started work by then. Sabina used to sleep in my room on Observatoriegatan when she got permission to stay out overnight. In the morning when I went to work, I gave her a tenner. When I came back she was sitting waiting for me on the pavement. And Edvard was still keeping an eye on me; once a month he checked my liver and kidneys and heart and helped me work out how much I could drink without them giving up. He would stand on the street in front of his Mercedes and sound the horn for me and he let me drive through Stockholm while he recorded my*

255

*levels. When Sabina went, he disappeared too. I never saw him*
*again.*

---

One afternoon, she was not waiting. A few days passed; he could smell her scent wafting past like a wound in the air, a moment instantly dispelled. Some weeks later she was found in the park out at Stora Skuggan, hanging alone on a rope under one of the gigantic oak trees. Jim rang Inger Vogel, who came over with her medical bag filled with pink pills. She stayed with him in his little rented room for the winter.

---

I bump into him outside his door when he is on his way to the corner shop in his dressing gown and slippers, to buy cigarettes and milk. He has Inger Vogel with him and smells faintly of old wine and something else, loneliness perhaps. Inger Vogel looks different; without her nurse's uniform she looks rounder, gentler, like any other woman. Shyly she touches my cheek, without meeting my eye.

"You don't need to worry about me, Jackie," Jim says. "Alcohol's a gift to a human being. You'll discover that for yourself one day."

"I didn't say I was worried," I say, and walk on down the street.

*

I am fourteen, fifteen, sixteen, and on my seventeenth birth-day Blenda sits opposite me in her pageboy cut, swirling a wine glass round in her hand.

"Jim always says you saved his life when you went to Beckomberga," she says. "I'm glad about that, I'm glad you saved him for me, Jackie."

Jim has married Blenda and they have had two sons. At night when the boys have gone to sleep, we drink together, sitting in their large living room with a view over Vasa Park.

When I reach eighteen I stop visiting them. When I ring their apartment no-one picks up and my letters go unanswered. They are either unhappy, or they have as much as they need with each other.

I am walking down the hill on Drottninggatan with some friends from university when Jim falls out of one of the pubs. He is wearing a torn, dark coat and stumbles in the snow several times before getting to his feet and drifting further into the city. It looks at one point as though he will not man-age to get up again, that he will just remain on the ground and let people step over him while the snow continues to fall.

"Poor bastard," Ylva whispers to me, pointing to Jim with-out knowing who he is, and we see his back slowly disappear into the crowd. I regret I did not go up to him and say hello, I should have held out my hand and helped him up out of the snow. I could have sat down next to him, brushed the snow from his hair, asked:

"Can you manage now?"

"Don't you want to stay for a while?"

"My lecture starts in ten minutes."

"Just sit with me for a few minutes. I'm not doing too well, Jackie. Where have you been all this time?"

"I rang several times, I wrote you letters, but you never wrote back."

"Didn't I?"

"No."

"How could I be so stupid that I threw away the best thing I had?"

"I don't know, Jim. I'm going now."

Marion is only a few weeks old when Jim phones out of the blue, from a taxi on the way to the airport. It has been nearly two decades. He is drunk and his voice is the same as it always was: warm, euphoric, close.

"You've had a boy?"

"Yes. Marion."

"Nice name. May I see him? May I hold him?"

"Do you want to?"

"Of course I want to. Have you been to Paris, Jackie?"

A fierce intake of breath as he lights a cigarette and the taxi driver's objections in the background, forcing him reluctantly to put it out. I wait. Marion has fallen asleep on my shoulder; I am standing in front of the bathroom mirror, speaking with the receiver clamped between my chin and shoulder, a tiny streak of milk is running down my bare arm.

"Weren't you allowed to smoke in the taxi?"

"No, I wasn't."

I smile at my reflection.

"Sad state of affairs."

"Yes, isn't it?"

His smile is audible down the telephone.

"I haven't got a hotel yet, but I took a chance and booked a flight for you too, Jackie. We can stay right by l'autoroute de l'Est with a view of the river, or by l'Opéra if you prefer. The trees are in leaf in the Tuileries Gardens now."

I did not take him up on the offer. On his return he rang and asked me to go over with Marion. The apartment by Vasa Park had been dismantled and packed into boxes; Blenda and the boys had moved out. There was no trace of them in the large, light rooms, just a little red musical box on a chair in the hall which one of them must have put down when he took off his jacket and then forgotten about.

Jim looked as though he had been drinking for months. He gazed at Marion for a long time, tentatively touched the downy hair on the top of his head, but did not dare hold him because his hands were shaking. Soon he would be moving the piano down to Cariño, he had found a little house by the ocean. He sat in his dressing gown on a packing crate and showed me lesions on his shoulders; they looked like the scars of wings that had been ripped off. He said he had fallen into a bonfire on a beach outside Biarritz. I washed the blood and sand out of the wounds and helped him into a clean T-shirt, and then we sat looking out at the night.

On the way out of the hospital gates, Lone stops. It is the last dream.

"What do you think about the hospital then? Why was everybody so scared of that place?"

"It's like vertigo, that fear of falling and being carried away into the night, of winding up on the outside. But there's nothing here to be afraid of."

"And you liked being here?"

"Yes, I liked being here very much. I liked Jim."

We carry on walking, slowly, over to the bus stop. A gentle winter rain falls on us, in the distance the sound of yet another aircraft on its descent over the treetops.

"And now?"

"Now the only thing left is the end."

"And how do you know when a story ends?"

"You just know."

Occasional snowflakes fall from the night sky and land like thin powder on the grass. I pull my jacket tighter around me.

"Lone, can you see that solitary star hanging above the trees over there?"

"Yes."

"When it falls, it's all over."

# III

# THE LAST CONVERSATION
# (ABOUT LONELINESS)

One night I see a star fall; it leaves a milk-white trail behind it in the night sky. And Jim writes to me again from Cariño; it reminds me of long childhood letters.

"I'm so lonely here, Jackie. I want you to know that this feels as though it will be the last lap. Don't be sad. You know how it is."

It is Jim's voice again on the telephone. Subdued and flat, it sounds as though it has been under water for quite some time.

"Listen Jackie . . ."

"Hello, Jim. How are you?"

"Lonely . . . Do you understand?"

"Yes."

I listen for the ocean in the background, but there is silence around him, as if he has finally shut the door that is always left open and which slams in the wind even at night, letting sand and snails and dead insects whirl into the Cariño house and leaving them in heaps against the walls. All that can be heard is the sound of a match being struck and the smoke leaving his mouth and dispersing over his lonely figure at the stone table in the living room.

"What are you thinking, Jackie?"

"I'm thinking that I've always been afraid of being sick."

"How do you mean, sick?"

"Mad."

"But you haven't been."

"Sometimes I wish it would happen just so I don't have to be afraid any longer."

All of a sudden his voice is utterly clear, soft, present, sober.

"But listen, you won't be sick. You'll be something else."

I look at the horizon blazing in the distance and the huge clouds illuminated by the last of the light.

"How do you know?"

He sits in silence for a long moment, and I hear only the sudden, violent intake of breath with every draw he takes on the cigarette.

"I don't know, Jackie. Before, I was always so scared you would take your own life, but now I'm not."

"Why not?"

"I always thought you'd be condemned to the same darkness as me, but I realise that's not the case. I only know it's different for you. I hope it's the same for Marion."

What do you do with a blessing like that, I think, as I sit in the night with twelve blue pearls in my hand, still waiting for life to take hold of me and whisk me away, still waiting for it to finally start.

"Don't wait," Jim says, as if he has read my thoughts. "Life never starts, it only ends. Suddenly. Just like that."

I hear him snap his fingers in the air and then we sit in

silence once again, with music in the background from the gramophone. Soft tones in the night, the last sounds from Cariño. I think about Marion when he was younger, how he would try to catch the aeroplanes in the sky between his finger and thumb, never understanding they were at such a vast distance, forever believing they were tiny toys he could hold in his hand.

"I always thought I could save you," I whisper, "but maybe it's not possible to save someone from himself. Perhaps you knew all the time it would never work, I just thought it was what you wanted."

Jim laughs quietly.

"Of course I bloody wanted it, Jackie, it's the only thing anyone wants. But it was impossible, it was futile. It wouldn't have made any difference, whatever you did."

"Wouldn't it?"

"No."

*

And then I hear the ocean once more, the great roar outside; he might have opened the door again and be standing by it, smoking.

"I'd like to ask you something, Jackie. That's why I rang. One last thing."

"Yes?"

"I'd like you to be with me at the end. If you could be with me on the beach when I walk out into the water, I wouldn't be so scared."

Sometimes, immediately before I fall asleep, pictures appear to me of the unmoving blue-toned trees above the exercise yard at Stora Mans. They are motionless despite the gentle breeze passing through Clock-House Park, as if nothing could ever disturb them. And I hear the clicking noise of little newts that collect in the ponds over spring; I see the glistening black rocks at Lake Judarn where we used to walk when Jim had permission to leave the hospital, where we could stand for hours on the steep side, where the water was always in shadow, looking at our shifting reflections far below.

Lone has always said my face and Jim's were chiselled with the same tool, and when I lie awake in the first light of dawn I see, in the photograph hanging above my bed of the three of us at Beckomberga, that I have in me both Jim's insatiability and Lone's solitude. And, as the birds awaken and the bells start to ring in Hedvig Eleonora Church, I can see them as they were at the beginning, at our family's start, when they were sauntering down Norrtullsgatan on their way to the university, each with a book under their arm. Lone in a suede jacket and high boots and Jim in a baggy corduroy suit. And now Jim bends to kiss her in front of the window of the antiques shop before they carry on down the street. A kiss that is a beginning, and a promise that he will break so many times. But in that second they are lit up with a forceful inner light, and their faces are tinged with gold from the shining sun behind Observatorie-lunden Park. A few gilded dragonflies that remain after the

270

summer spin around them still, they fly with Jim and Lone into the blinding light of the future, and I hear Jim's drunken voice on the telephone from Cariño.

"I'm actually incredibly grateful that I was sick. I wouldn't have understood anything of the world otherwise."

"When are you going to go, Jim?"

"I can't say."

"Will you be thinking of me when you swim off?"

"I don't think I'll be thinking about anything."

"Will you ring me?"

"If you like."

"Just one last question."

"Yes?"

"Did you ever love me?"

"I don't know, Jackie. I don't know whether I did."

# THE LAST PATIENT
# (STILL IN THE LIGHT)

*And one fine day people will stand there and ask: Was this really a change for the better, or might I have been mistaken?*

It is dark outside now. Olof has stopped weeping and sits with his large cotton handkerchief on his knee.

"One last thing, Doctor."

"Shoot."

"It was sane people who killed Jesus, wasn't it?"

Dr Janowski laughs softly.

"You're right there, Olof. It was sane people who killed Jesus."

"Yes, I thought so."

A wind blows down the corridors outside. Olof stands up, listening for a tune.

"Can you hear, Doctor Janowski?"

"No, I can't hear anything."

Olof shushes him.

"Can't you hear it?"

"No, just the wind."

"It's not the wind. It's that choir again. They're singing for me. They're singing for us. Can you really not hear?"

Dr Janowski gets to his feet and listens.

"What are they singing?"

"I can't say."

"Sing it then."

Olof sings.

*

In the winter of 1995 the last ward at Beckomberga closes. Dr Janowski wanders slowly down the darkened corridors before opening the door to the winter light. He stands for a while under the gold inscription, looking out over the small frozen pond. Then he buttons up his overcoat and walks down the lime tree avenue.

---

During the whole of the 1980s patients are removed from mental hospitals as a consequence of criticism of the care provided in them, and as part of the wave of deinstitutionalisation sweeping across the western world. Antipsychotic drugs appearing in the 1960s make it possible to live outside institutions and the enormous financial resources the old mental hospitals consumed are no longer available.

Psychiatric care now happens within large general hospitals. Only about ten per cent of the former beds still remain.

Sometimes it has seemed to me that Beckomberga's age coincided with the age of the welfare state, 1932 to 1995.

ET MISERICORDIA

Today, when I crossed the square, I saw the sailor again for the first time in weeks. He sat in his usual place, a bottle of aquavit in one hand, but in a wheelchair now. Both his legs had been amputated just below the groin, the dressings were still on. When he saw me he waved and shouted and I sat down on the bench next to him.

"What happened to your legs?" I asked, faint with nausea and trying not to look at his mutilated lower body; it looked as though he had been through a war. He threw up his hands and laughed.

"They're gone."

"Yes, I can see, but what happened to them?"

"Oh, those legs never took me anywhere decent anyway. They've always gone wherever they wanted. You know, straight to the first available off-licence or to the square here. You know how it is. And I've got these great things now,." He smiled, tapping the chair's narrow wheels.

I went to collect Marion afterwards, crying all the way, it felt as though I had just been to a funeral. When I entered the nursery he rushed through the little rooms towards me. He is equally, unimaginably happy every time, and so am I. It is like a current of air inside me, a possibility, a chink in the darkness.

*

Immediately before Marion was born, a little bird flew into the delivery room as I stood naked under the open hospital robe. The burning pain in my pelvis was so strong it had erased all my thoughts, wiped out my fear of being torn apart like a piece of cloth and of bleeding to death. The bird was as small as a hummingbird and bright blue. Sitting in the open window, watching me, it gave me the impression that I was chosen, and maybe I was. Like a little dolphin Marion came out of me. It happened so quickly he nearly hit the floor before I caught him. Afterwards I thought of Lone, that she must have done the same thing for me so long ago. She was alone in the delivery room too; Jim had not come home that night and did not appear in the hospital until morning, drunk and with an armful of roses so large the staff had to bring out buckets. In the only photograph from the hospital, Lone looks furious, defeated, sitting on the edge of the bed and holding me for the first time. Her make-up has run and made black streaks under her eyes.

I often think about Rickard, how gentle he was with me, I think of his hands, how they held my hands above my head when we made love, how he stroked my palm so lightly with his fingers, to and fro along my life line and up over the thin veins in my wrist. I think he should have held me tighter, never let me go. When Marion was only a few months old, he rang from Helsinki and wept. I did not know what to say, so I put the receiver down and then lay next to it on the floor and listened to him cry. After a while he hung up, perhaps he figured out I was no longer there.

Sometimes I think Paul rescued me from happiness, I do not think I could have coped with it. Once we came close to it, on Kammakargatan in the afternoons when we were alone in the world, lying in the sunshine on Lone's big bed. It was like an ache within, as if I would overflow and tip up inside, an inward somersault.

It is late summer now and the proper people are back in the city, filling it with their sounds, with their affluence and self-belief, their jogging routes. The wig-maker down here has closed indefinitely, the slip of paper with "Back Soon" has been there for weeks, and in the baptistery of the church they have taken the feather-child out of the glass coffin. When I awake in the mornings I do not know whether I am still young and waiting for life to begin, or whether everything was over long ago, but when I stretch out my hand Marion is lying there, wrapped in sheets. I know he is awake, even though he is facing the other way.

"I dreamt of Granddad," he says, his voice husky with sleep.

"What did you dream?" I ask.

"That he cycled right out into the sea. Has he gone now?"

"No, Jim's still there. He's in his house by the beach."

"How long will he be there?"

"I don't know. He doesn't know either."

"And then?"

"Then he'll come here and visit us."

He turns to look at me and his eyes are wide open, the pupils bottomless, and it seems as if an ocean current flows deep inside him.

"Do you think he will?"

The wind plays with the white voile curtain at the window and I think the only thing Jim has ever given me is his way of always telling it like it is, even when it hurts, as now.

"I don't know, Marion," I say finally. "I believe that most of all he wants to go away."

"Has he always?"

"I think so."

"But he's old now, isn't he?"

"Yes, but sometimes you can be young on the inside, even though you look old."

"Do you wish you could, Mum?"

"Be gone?"

"Yes."

"No, I don't. I want to be here with you."

The curtain is sucked out of the window and then slackens, as if the wind will never touch it again. I reach out and touch Marion's cheek with my hand, just as Jim used to touch my cheek a long time ago, fleetingly, like a bird's wing.

"What are you thinking about, Marion?"

"I'm thinking about all the fun we're going to have."

I laugh.

"What are we going to do?"

"You'll see."

———∞———

In my memory white ocean birds fly along the hospital corridors. It cannot have been like that, but it is how I remember it the first time we visit him. The sound of rustling feathers and wings and the faint smell of sea and death, as if waves are breaking on a shore somewhere inside the building, as if the architecture conceals an open wound.

We wandered around in the beautiful hospital park for a while before we took the bus back into the city. A week later we were there again. The park was in bloom, the sky appeared to be sinking, it was so low, and the flowers were as big as my head. Japanese cherry blossom trees and silver trees that had been planted at some time in the infancy of the welfare state, climbing roses over sun-bleached walls, and I stood there looking up at the many eyes of the enormous building looking at us. And when I touched Jim he jumped, as if I had rubbed a sore.

"Hello, sweetie."

"What made you fall?"

"I don't know. Suddenly a heaven opened up under the earth. I just threw myself in."

It was the crowns of the enormous trees that obscured Jim and me as we walked hand in hand through the hospital gardens, the big shadow that hastened over the burnt black grass when a large cloud scudded past above. That shadow is my fear of the night, my fear of being confined, of being loved, of losing Marion. I think of the nights when I woke next to Rickard and was afraid of something I could never explain in the light of day, a sudden pressure in my head, right next to my cochlea, an unrelenting, deafening thunder, like the roar of a forest fire in the distance, or a sun that shines unexpectedly at night, that makes your thoughts run riot. And the fear is Paul and the birds of prey hovering up high above the hospital building and the flowers as tall as a man at the back of Stora Mans; the fear is the massive roots that glowed like a fire at dusk in Judarn Forest. Olof Palme has just become prime minister for the second time and every morning on his way from his home in Vällingby to Rosenbad he drives past Beckomberga to visit his mother. And when he walks under the great trees in Clock-House Park he is nobody, just a man on his own going to visit an old woman in a mental hospital. Inside the ward she trots towards him like a child, an elderly girl who hurries along the corridors, no longer remembering who he is, only that he is the nice man wearing a suit and carrying a briefcase who turns up every morning and sits with her for a while before he disappears back down the corridor. And the fear is Lone who sits on the balcony in the sun with a book and waits for Marion and me. The fear is Jim's face when the sun shines upon it; and that is also where the fear stops, in the mellow sunlight when he makes someone burst into laughter in the huddle of men smoking in the shadow of Stora Mans. And the instant Jim sees me, his face brightens.

"Is it you again, little nutcase?"

The fear is also Sabina running through the forest in the fur coat with a pack of guard dogs after her, it is the birds and dragonflies and spruce trees and the blood-red marks on her calves afterwards, her naked body in the morgue, it is the patients without families who float in huge concrete vats filled with formaldehyde in the medical school.

"All I ask is freedom and when freedom is denied me, I take it anyway," she says.

"And if it's you who falls, Sabina?"

For her, insanity is hope, that is what I always forget.

"So be it. To fall is to understand the universe."

The words are her rosary. The magic power they held for her was like the power of prayer, pearl after pearl attached to a thread of light in her darkness. I look at her lost pearls on the windowsill. I look at my own face reflected in the unlit bed-room window. And when I close my eyes I can hear the mighty waves of the Atlantic, how they crash in over the beaches and slowly pull back out to sea; they are like breathing, like infinitely slow heartbeats, like an eye that opens and closes, like night pouring in over the planet. I hold the pearls next to my heart while I wait for Jim to ring from Cariño and ask me to go to him. The pearls are my amulet against the immense night that is approaching.

\*

285

*Jim: I imagine I'm standing on a trampoline, looking down into the water. Then I make the perfect jump and disappear into the deep. A few seconds later the surface is a black mirror once again. It will be as if I have never been here. And there is no rope that holds us to the earth, no tie binding the moon to the earth. So what could make me stay? What would join me to the world if not a rope, if not love? But such a thing does not exist, and never has.*

———oooo———

I used to observe Lone and him when they lay sleeping in the mornings on Kammakargatan, entangled in the damp sheets, swathed in the blaze of light filtering through the window. Lone always held a pillow to her stomach in her sleep and the tiny gold heart vibrated at her throat. It was as if I truly believed my gaze could protect them, that I could wrap them in my blessing and shield them from the approaching darkness, from the clouds that had been gathering on the horizon for some time, rolling in over the sky and colliding with one another. I thought my gaze could keep them in the light forever; I always imagined I possessed a superhuman strength. I do not know where the idea came from. I have never saved anyone, never been close to saving anyone.

THIS NOVEL IS DEDICATED TO ALL THOSE WHO PASSED THROUGH THE HOSPITAL PARK AT BECKOMBERGA OVER THE YEARS 1932 TO 1995.

SARA STRIDSBERG is a writer and playwright living in Stockholm. Her second novel, *The Faculty of Dreams* (forthcoming in 2017), was winner of the Nordic Council Literature Prize, and her novels have four times been shortlisted for Sweden's August Prize. *The Gravity of Love – Ode to My Family*, has been sold in fifteen languages and was the 2015 Swedish winner of the European Prize for Literature.

DEBORAH BRAGAN-TURNER is the translator from Swedish of works by P. O. Enquist and Anne Swärd.